First Kisses, Near Misses

Short Stories from the World of Cindy Eller

Elizabeth A Reeves

Copyright © 2014

Dedication

These stories are dedicated to those who believe in love, despite the odds, despite the world, and believe in loving with every breath and with unfailing, unflinching courage.

How (Not) to Kiss (at all)

Kade Michaels was the most beautiful person I had ever seen. I knew it wasn't the thing to call a guy beautiful, but that's what he was. With dark black hair that always seemed to fall into his bluer-than-blue eyes, which featured the longest black eyelashes I had ever seen—he was beautiful. There was no other word for it.

I'd tried to ignore my growing interest in him all school year. For one thing, I had a huge, serious secret hanging over my head.

I was the only person in my entire high school that was a witch.

I'm not talking Wicca, and I'm not even talking about all those other imitations out there. I was the real thing—a Magical being. I actually wasn't allowed to use the term 'witch'. My mother, who was practically a mind-reader, would have had a conniption if she knew I secretly, in the very back recesses of my brain, considered myself that. No, I was supposed to call myself a 'Magical Practitioner'.

I sat up straight in my chair in the middle of Algebra. Knowing that Kade Michaels was sitting directly behind me made it impossible to relax. Sometimes I could swear I could feel his breath on the back of my neck. Even the thought of that made me get all tingly and sweaty all at once—like I could giggle or throw up or do something drastic all at once.

Kade was by far the best part of being dropped from yet another Magical school and being forced to relocate to an Ordinary high school. Gone were my Magical history classes—mostly about the barrier and how it had been erected and all that fun stuff. No more nearly blowing my teachers up in potions. No, my defunct and practically non-existent Magic and I had been banished to the nearest Ordinary high school so quickly I was sure there had been plenty of Magic involved in the transfer.

Nothing could have prepared me for the culture shock of switching schools partway through the year from a relatively sheltered Magical all-girls academy, to a sprawling urban high school complete with 'his' and 'hers' bathrooms.

And Kade Michaels.

Ever since my sister, Goldie, had decided to tape up all the pages from my last math notebook—complete with all my doodles that may or may not have referred to myself as 'Mrs. Kade Michaels' all over the family house, I'd had to keep my urge to doodle under wraps. I wouldn't put it past my little sister to find a way to humiliate me at my new school, even if she was acceptable to the Magical community.

Unlike me.

Little sisters were definitely on my 'things that bug me' list. As well as my mother, my school... pretty much everything. I spent an awful lot of time being bugged. I knew that was part of being a teenager, but that didn't keep me from being pissed off that my life was nuts. Life wasn't fair.

And I hated that my brain was running on clichés.

My already stiff back stiffened further as I felt a finger poke into my shoulder. I jumped, not sure if it had been on purpose. After a moment I felt a tug on my long, true-red hair. I glanced over my shoulder.

Kade was holding a thin slip of paper out toward me.

I glanced at our math teacher. As usual, he wasn't paying attention to anything the class was doing. I reached over my shoulder to take the little triangle of paper.

I looked down at it for a moment.

I'd had notes passed to me before, of course. When I was in first grade I'd even passed notes back and forth with Sammy Eller during our French classes. I'd had this crazy idea that we were going to grow up and marry each other because we shared the same last name. How cool would it be not to have to change my last name when I got married?

I'd also been on the receiving end of the other side of the spectrum of notes. I'd had anonymous notes that had been so hurtful that the only recourse had been to flush them down the school toilets or take them home and watch them burn.

My sisters had found one of those at one time and doled out some serious witch-style justice.

But that had been at Magic school.

My fingers picked at the folds of the note. I un-creased them slowly, reluctant to see what was inside. My heart pounded in my throat. I swallowed hard.

Hey, I read. *I wanna talk to you later. You game? K*

I glanced over my shoulder at Kade.

He nodded and grinned. He had super-straight teeth—the kind that spoke of years in braces.

Oh, gosh. Now I was staring at his mouth. Smooth move, Cindy.

I managed to bob my head in a little nod before I turned back around.

I thought I might throw up. What if he just wanted to meet me to say something mean? Why would he want to talk to me, anyway? It wasn't like I was pretty, or smart, or even Magical—not that he could ever EVER know about me having Magic. Why would someone like Kade Michaels want to talk to me?

The bell rang and I swept my books off of my desk and right into my backpack.

I guessed I was about to find out. School was out for the day.

I never would have guessed that I'd be longing for another half-hour of math.

"Hey." I whirled around to face Kade as he slung his arm casually over my shoulders, backpack and all. He grinned down at me. I'd never realized just how tall he was, but he towered over my five foot two frame.

"Hi," I said shyly.

"You want to go somewhere and talk?" He took my bag from me before I could even answer, which was a good thing, as I apparently had forgotten how to talk.

I managed to nod, though part of me wanted to grab my bag and hightail out of there. I paused. "I'll miss the bus," I managed to say.

"I'll drive you home," Kade said easily. "Is that OK?"

It was better than OK. I felt the corners of my mouth turn up at the idea. Kade Michaels was going to drive me home?

Hold on, Kade Michaels was going to drive me home. I couldn't let that happen. No way could I let my mother know that I'd been hanging out with an Ordinary boy outside of school. She would freak. And when my mom freaked out things happened—things like earthquakes.

Kade must have sensed my reluctance. "It's OK, isn't it?" I looked up at his face. There was a line between his eyes. I thought I might have hurt his feelings or something.

"It's fine," I said quickly. "My mom's just a little... strange."

"Oh, one of those," Kade said, his voice understanding. "How about I drop you off at the corner, then?"

I grinned again, this time in relief. "Why are you being so nice?" The words blurted out before I could even gather together a coherent thought. I immediately wanted to slap my forehead or dig out a section of the sidewalk to hide in.

"Isn't it clear? I like you, Cindy." He tugged gently on one of my wild, red curls, smiling down at me as if he liked what he saw.

"You do?" Yet again I was saying the worst thing possible.

But I didn't know how to do this. No boy had ever liked me enough to want to risk association with my mother. After all, she was the strongest Earth witch of her generation. She was a formidable woman. That sort of thing tended to keep the crushes at bay.

Of course, Kade didn't know any of that stuff. As far as I knew, I was just as Ordinary as he was.

As if it were the most natural thing in the world, Kade reached out and took my hand in his. His hands were bigger than mine, and dry, while I was afraid mine were sweaty. I didn't want to gross him out, but he didn't seem to notice. He just laced his fingers between mine and let our arms swing between us. It was nice. Shivery tingles raced up my arm, making my heart thud.

I was holding hands with Kade Michaels. Me. Awkward, Magically impotent Cindy Eller was holding hands with the most beautiful boy in the entire universe.

Was the world about to end?

Maybe I was dreaming.

I looked sideways at the boy I was walking with.

If this was a dream, I never wanted to wake up again.

From then on that's just the way it was. I walked in a dream. Overnight I'd gone from that strange girl with the red hair to Kade Michael's girlfriend. We did everything together. He met me at the bus stop every morning to drive me to school and dropped me off every afternoon on the corner closest to my house. When I was with him I felt like a completely different person. My insecurities seemed to whisper in my ears, instead of screaming all day long in my head.

Finally, here was someone who thought I was good enough.

"You know," he said, wrapping one of my curls around his finger. "You are truly beautiful, Cindy Eller."

I thought my heart my burst, I was so happy.

"You're coming to prom with me, right?" He grinned at my expression.

I couldn't stop staring at him. "Uh," I managed.

"Cool," he said. "I can't wait to see you all dressed up and gorgeous."

I winced. I hated to tell him, but all the dresses and makeup and Magic in the world wasn't going to make me gorgeous.

"Hey, none of that," he said gently. When I blinked at him he continued. "You wear your thoughts on your face, Cindy." He leaned toward me. For a breathless moment I thought he was about to kiss me. "You're beautiful, Cindy. You don't have to believe me, because it's not about me or you. It's just fact. You can't argue with fact."

"Kade," I said, feeling my face burn. One of the perks of being a redhead was that my face turned bright red every time I blushed.

"Just wait," he whispered in my ear. "We're going to have the best prom ever. You'll see."

He leaned back and I remembered to breathe again.

Suddenly, I couldn't wait for prom.

Of course, going to prom with Kade meant that I had to come clean with my mom and my sisters. They all wanted to meet him, but I managed to hold out. There was no way I was going to let them scare him off before prom. They would just have to wait until after.

"I bet he's a toad," I heard Iris whispered to Goldie. "I bet he has warts."

I just grinned to myself. Kade Michaels was just perfect. And soon my entire family was going to see it, too.

Two hours before we were supposed to meet for prom, I was ready to call the whole thing off. There was no way I was ever going to be able to get ready in time. Here I was, Cindy Eller, but there was no Faerie godmother in sight. My hair was standing straight up on end, my dress had somehow gotten a long rip in one side, and I'd managed to stab myself in the eye with my mascara wand no less than six times.

"It takes talent," I grumbled, "to be as disastrous a person as I am! What kind of girl can't even get dressed?"

"Calm down," Rose said. My sister who was closest in age to me was pretty enough to make Helen in Troy seem plain. With her dark hair and blood-red lips, she was considered the beauty in a family of gorgeous young ladies.

All except for me.

"I'll help you," Rose said soothingly. Which one of us was supposed to be the big sister anyway? Rose patched up my dress with a literal snap of her fingers. She was as talented Magically as she was beautiful.

Life was so unfair.

With my dress repaired, it was time to try to fix up the walking disaster that was me. My wild red curls defied all attempts to tame it. Rose actually broke one curling iron, and two brushes lost so many bristles they looked like they'd been chewed by a dog.

She sighed. "I guess we'll just have to embrace the madness," she said, "since it refuses to be tamed."

"Oh, no," I exclaimed. "I'm not going to prom with eight-foot high and eighteen foot wide hair. I'd rather not go than utterly humiliate myself like that."

"Relax," she said, opening a drawer and pulling out a vial of something that smelled strongly of roses. I had a hunch it was one of her experimental herbal concoctions. "Just trust me."

"It's not like I have a choice," I muttered. I leaned back and even dozed off as Rose fussed over every strand of my hair.

By the time she nudged me awake my hair had been tamed... sort of. It was still wildly curly and fell past my butt, but now each curl was defined, and looked purposely designed.

Sleek and sexy it was not, but it was a billion times better than my usual chaos.

"You're the best," I told Rose, squeezing her so hard she started to squirm.

"Thank me later," she said grimly. "Now I'm going to put your makeup on you."

If Rose ever went out for a career as a Faerie godmother, I was going to strongly recommend her.

"Wow," Kade said, as I made my way down the stairs to greet him. It would have been like something out of a fairytale if I hadn't been struggling so hard not to trip on the hem of my skirt and fall flat on my face. I was already feeling a little pinched and prodded, the last thing I needed was a black eye on top of everything else.

That 'wow' made it all worth it.

"Wow, yourself," I answered, admiring his tuxedo. He should have looked ridiculous in full dress attire like that, but he didn't. He looked super handsome and suave.

He offered me his arm. "Shall we?"

I sniggered. "We shall, Sirrah."

I'd never ridden in a limo before, but I didn't even really notice it on the way to the dance. I was too aware of the way Kade was staring at me. I was actually relieved to jump out of the vehicle before we got to the dance. Maybe once we were there, we'd be able to talk and act like normal.

Our prom was held in the ballroom of a nice hotel. The place was loud and crowded, not usually my cup of tea. With Kade's hand on my elbow we wove our way through the crush and found a little niche on the dance floor where I could put my arms around his neck and pretend I knew how to slow dance.

"There you guys are." I practically jumped as Laura and Brian, two of Kade's best friends, bumped into us. Laura looked cute and dainty in her pale pink dress. It highlighted the strawberry blond of her hair and made her look angelic, which was, as far as I could tell, as far from the truth as possible. Laura was always getting into some kind of scrape at school. She had a creative mind and no sense of boundaries.

"Kade," she said, grabbing him by the elbow. "I've always wanted to get Tacos in a limo. Please, can we all go in yours? It will be super fun!"

Kade looked down at me, raising his eyebrows.

I shrugged. I didn't mind what we did, as long as I got to be with Kade. I wasn't overly attached to being at the prom. I didn't know Laura and Brian that well, but I figured there couldn't be any harm in the four of us hopping into the limo and getting some Tacos from a drive through.

In fact, it sounded kind of silly and fun, not like anything I would usually do.

Kade wrapped his arm around me as we made our way out to the parking lot to where the limo was waiting for us. I crawled into the farthest seat while Laura and Brian settled together closest to the doors.

"Gosh, I feel like a super model or a movie star," Laura gushed, pretending to look at me over a pair of imaginary sunglasses. "Isn't this just too exciting?" She turned toward Brian and batted her eyelashes at him. "Can't you see me riding in one of these all the time?"

His response was to practically eat her face off. I had never seen two people in real life kiss like this. It was less like romance and more like a zombie horror flick.

"Guys," Kade said, sighing as if this were all-too common of an occurrence. "Come on, we're not even out of the parking lot yet."

Something about the tonsil-swapping going on feet away from us made me super aware of Kade sitting there, with his thigh brushing against mine. What was Kade thinking right now? Did he expect me to crawl all over him like Laura was with Brian?

"Wow, you guys look uncomfortable," Laura commented, when she came up for air enough to bounce on the back seat and look out the windows. "What, it's not like you guys have never kissed or anything, have you?"

I felt, more than saw, Kade not looking at me. It was mutual, because I was very much not looking at him.

"Oh, my gosh," Laura said, her baby blue eyes widening to the point that it looked like they might just pop out of their sockets. "What are you waiting for? It's not like the nineteen hundreds, people. Unless..." her eyes narrowed at me. "You're not Amish, are you?"

I choked. "No."

She thought about that. "Lesbian?"

I stared at her.

"Huh," she said. "Go figure. I don't get it. You two are both attractive and all. Obviously you like each other. What's been holding you back?"

I wasn't about to tell her that Kade was the first guy I'd ever gone out with or that the whole idea of kissing him made me feel like I was going to pass out or throw up or, worse of all, both.

"Well," she said, "I think you should kiss right now."

"Dude," Brian said. "Do it."

Kade looped his arm around my shoulders. I froze. I could feel myself go stiff. I hoped he wasn't going to try to go in for the kiss. Not now. Not like this. I wanted our first kiss to be special... not one of those 'peer pressure' moments my mother had driven over and over into my brain.

He looped his fingers in mine and just leaned back, his body totally relaxed.

"Shut up, Laura," he said, evenly. There was no malice in his voice whatsoever.

She rolled her eyes, then bounced as she looked out of the window. "Yay! We're here!"

Our poor driver had to keep backing the whole limo up just to make the turn into the drive thru. I wondered if he'd had to do something like this before. I wondered how much of his time was spent shuttling around stupid kids who just wanted to flaunt the fact that they were in a limo and could play around with it.

And then, once we were ready to order, all Laura wanted was a diet coke.

"We should have stayed at the dance," Kade whispered in my ear.

I turned to smile at him. I'd just been thinking the same thing.

He pulled me closer and tucked me under his chin, wrapping both arms around me as the limo did a u-turn to take us back to the prom.

Laura and Brian used all the time left in the limo to go zombie on each other again.

I studied my toenail polish so I could ignore them. I didn't mind public affection or kissing. This was just... way beyond gross. If they actually ended up being zombies, I didn't think I had enough Magic to keep me and Kade safe.

I couldn't get back to the prom fast enough, especially if that meant our zombie friends would eat other people before us. I wasn't above using a human shield or two. There were a few people our high school would be fine without, I was sure.

"That was so stupid," Kade said, as he helped me back out of the limo. I was grateful for his hands, as getting out of the vehicle in a dress was a lot more difficult than elegant.

Who was I kidding? I wasn't cut out for all this elegance stuff. I was more the walking disaster type.

Kade played with one of my curls. "How about we find another song to slow dance to?" His breath brushed my cheek at the suggestion. I felt goose bumps pop up all over my arms.

We walked back into the hotel arm in arm, heading for the ballroom. There was a fountain in the foyer—one of those 'make a wish' kind, full of pennies and other coins. I swore I could see a Canadian loony in there somewhere. I wondered how many different currencies could be found in a fountain like this one.

"Wait," Kade said. "I want to make a wish." He dug into his pocket, his other arm around me, and fished around until he came up with a quarter. He grinned at me as he flipped the coin into the air. It sparkled briefly under the lights before dipping down toward the water.

Before it even reached the surface he dipped down his head and kissed me.

There was nothing about the kiss that should have been special. What was the deal with kisses anyway? Lips touching lips, how could that fill me to overflowing with a fuzzy warms and a giddy rush all at once? My skin tingled. All the way down to my sparkling toenails I felt alive.

It was my first kiss. I couldn't have imagined a better one.

I opened my eyes and looked at him.

Kade gagged, choked, and clutched his hands to his face. His skin was taking on a peculiar shade of... blue? Green? Before my eyes his entire figure shifted and swam, and then he vanished.

"Kade?" I shrieked. "Oh, my gosh! Kade?"

All that was left of my date was a puddle of his tuxedo on the floor where he had been standing. I grappled through it, as if I could find some reason for his disappearance in the folds of fabric.

Something... moved.

I bit back another shriek as something tiny moved again, appearing out of one of the arms of the tuxedo's jacket.

It was a toad. A tiny, green, toad.

"K...Kade?" My voice wavered. Much as I wanted to believe otherwise, my gut told me that this little toad was my boyfriend. "Kade?"

He made a croaking sound. I jumped.

I bit my lip as I tried to scrape together the wild chaos that was rampaging through my brain. I had to get him back, but how? My first thought was that I had to kiss him back. That's what the princess in the stories always did, right? I lifted him up on my hands, said a brief prayer that he wasn't a toxic type of toad, and pressed my lips against his tiny warty side.

Nothing. He blinked at me and croaked again. This time there was no mistaking his tone. Kade was pissed off at me.

OK, so more kissing wasn't going to solve this problem. Maybe I could get my Magic to pull together enough to fix this. I closed my eyes, focusing as hard as I could. As usual, the particles of my Magic fought my attempt to direct them. I gathered together what I could and pushed the power toward the little toad that was Kade, focusing all my thoughts on his beautiful smile, on those gorgeous bluer-than-blue eyes.

I opened my eyes and there he was.

Still a toad.

Just a blue one.

"No," I wailed. I didn't want to bring my mom into this, but I knew I couldn't handle it on my own. I grabbed up the toad that was Kade and his clothes and ran for the nearest exit.

The tingling in my hand was the only warning I had. I put Kade down just in time to see him pop back into his normal, human self.

His normal, stark naked, self.

"What the hell?" he demanded, throwing himself backward from me. "What the hell was that, Cindy?"

"I don't know," I stammered. "I didn't mean..."

"You gave me something, didn't you?" His face was white as he grabbed up his clothes and held them in front of him.

He ducked back into the shadows, where no one would be able to see him. "Tell me the truth, you drugged me!"

"I did not," I protested. "I didn't drug you... I swear!"

"What the hell are you?" he demanded. I had turned my back, but I could hear him getting dressed. "What did you do to me?"

"I told you, I don't know!" My voice was rising to the point of hysteria.

He grabbed my shoulders and I looked into his blue eyes. They were hard and livid, his face turning purple. "You changed me into a toad? Tell me that you didn't change me into a toad."

"I—I can't," I whispered.

He dropped my arms as if they had burned him. "Get away from me," he said harshly. "*Witch.*"

I had never heard one word filled with such hatred, such loathing. I turned away from Kade and ran as fast as I could. I didn't care where I ended up, just as long as I never had to see Kade ever again.

I flipped on the mixer on the counter in front of me and watched as the butter and sugar spun together to become something full of promise. I leaned on one hand as I watched the ingredients combine.

My thoughts had been on Kade all day. Maybe because he had been my first—my first love, my first toad.

My first heartbreak.

After prom, Kade had done everything in his power to put me through hell. Only transferring schools and a mind-wipe via my mother had gotten him to stop threatening me and persecuting me, no matter where I went.

My first love had been my first hate. It was all very Romeo and Juliet.

Maybe I'd been thinking about him because of the new man in my life. I'd never really given up believing that someday I would find the one—the man I would kiss that wouldn't immediately turn into a toad.

Maybe Timothy would be that one.

I broke off a chunk of a cookie, still warm from the oven and lifted it into the air in a toast. "Here's to you, Kade, wherever you are—you really were a toad."

Of Love and Centaurs

"You're just jealous," I told my twin sister Starrie as she glowered at me from under her bangs. At times like this I liked to think of her as my evil twin, something that would have amused her to no end.

I decided not to share that thought with her.

She made a face at me. "I'm not jealous... ok, I am seriously jealous. You have a date with a centaur?"

I nodded.

"How did you even manage that?" Starrie demanded. "I mean, you're too shy to even talk to guys."

I shrugged. "Maybe it's different with centaurs."

We laughed together. We had the exact same laugh. In fact, we had the exact same everything, down to the swirls in our fingerprints and the two freckles on our left shoulders. Ordinary twins weren't as identical as we were.

Sometimes I envied them.

Don't get me wrong—I loved my sister and being twins with her. I loved that we could share thoughts sometimes and that even our own mother couldn't tell us apart when we swapped places. I loved knowing that I was never alone.

But sometimes I needed a little space. A little me time.

Starrie could be... exhausting. She was high-maintenance, hence the whole evil-twin thing.

"Oh, Mom is going to be so mad when she finds out," Starrie said suddenly, grinning at the idea of getting Mom's goat, yet again. I think it was her goal in life to drive Mom crazy. I figured, if our three older sisters hadn't managed to drive mom over the edge, the two of us weren't going to be able to pull it off.

"Mom can't find out," I said urgently. "Sister swear me that she won't find out."

Starrie grimaced, but looped her little finger through mine. "Fine. Sister swear." She pouted, tucking her deep black hair behind her ear at the same moment I did. "You have all the luck. I want a centaur."

"I'll find out if he has a brother," I promised.

"You could have found out before you went out with him," Starrie's pout deepened. She was really starting to feel sorry for herself now.

I rolled my eyes. "Look, I'm sorry, OK? Are you going to help me get ready for my date or not?"

I wished I could hide from Starrie how nervous I was about this date. She ignored all of the worked up energy coming in waves off of me, but I could feel her own energy reach out and try to soothe me.

It was nice of her, but did we really have to share everything? Did she really have to feel everything I was feeling? Couldn't I just keep my emotions private—just this once?

"I think you should wear that midnight top over those black shiny pants I bought," Starrie said, digging into her Magical purse, which carried pretty much all of her belongings in it. "You're going to go... riding, right?" She raised her eyebrows suggestively.

I giggled. "Starrie, you are so bad! But you're right, I should probably wear pants... and boots?"

What did a girl wear on a date with a centaur anyway? Dressage riding clothes? Cowgirl boots? I snorted at the idea.

"So," Starrie said. "Tell me all about this guy. What's he like? I can't believe you met him at the library!"

I grinned. I'd been researching a spell in the Magic Central library when I had, quite literally, run into the centaur's chest... his very bare chest. My face still burned at the memory.

"Maybe you'd pick up more guys if you actually went to the library once in a while," I teased, digging into my own purse for my midnight-blue nail polish. Some girls had fancy eye shadows or a thing for lip gloss—mine was nail polish. There was something soothing about brushing on a few coats of glossy colors that made me feel special and unique— something that was difficult to do when I had a twin sister like mine.

Starrie pouted. "Sorry that I was at the potions shop. I was trying to get the attention of that new employee... you know, the guy with the red hair?" She sighed.

I grinned to myself. Starrie had a thing for 'ginger' guys. Actually, I didn't mind a redhead myself, especially if that redhead was tall, muscular, and half-equine with an unbelievably adorable accent. He sounded like he was straight off the Scottish moors.

I sighed. So dreamy.

"I'll try to get you a date with a centaur," I promised, carefully brushing on a coat of polish. "I'm sure there are other... studs in the herd."

We glanced at each other and cracked up. I had to put my polish down before it ended up all over the floor.

"Studs?" Starrie gasped. "Rainey! That's just too good!"

I giggled. "Oh, my gosh, Starrie. He's so cute. I don't know why I said yes. It was like I couldn't help myself. I don't even know what centaurs do on a date. Do you?"

Starrie pursed her lips as she thought about it. I thought that expression made her look just like Mom, though I would never tell her that. It would have made her furious.

I really hoped she hadn't caught that thought.

After a moment, she shook her head. "I have no idea." She clapped her hands together. "I bet you're going to go for a long ride on the beach in the moonlight..." She sighed romantically.

I echoed her sigh. Even the thought of a date like that made my insides get all tingly and squishy. I felt like there were man-eating butterflies in there, trying to get out.

"I think I'm going to be sick," I told my twin.

Starrie grabbed me by the shoulders. "You aren't going to get sick," she told me, giving me a little shake. "You aren't going to get shy or nervous, got it? You're going to go out there and have a great time!"

I gave her a weak smile. "What would I ever do without you?"

"Oh, I don't know," Starrie said airily. "Probably sit in your room all day reading or drawing in your journal."

"Hey," I protested. "That's supposed to be a secret!"

Starrie shook her head. "Rainey, Rainey, Rainey. When are you going to learn that you can have no secrets from me?"

I snorted.

Sadly, she was right.

To calm my nerves I picked up my polish and set back to painting my nails again.

"Here," Starrie said, laying the outfit she had put together across the foot of my bed. "You can wear my good-luck charm earrings."

"Really?" I gasped as I looked at the beautiful, entwined pewter charms that Starrie had been hoarding for a special occasion. "Are you sure?"

She shrugged. "Sure, why not? You having a date with a centaur is almost the same as me having a date with him."

Starrie could be generous and understanding like that. It was one of the things I loved the most about her.

I stood in the middle of Magic Central, staring at my date, and decided that there could be no manlier creature in the world than a centaur. Everything about him was masculine—from his hard-core abs to his flowing red hair and the sheer power of his equine hindquarters. He was every girl's fantasy, and he was standing right in front of me.

"Hi, Drostan," I said shyly, trying not to ogle his bare chest and broad shoulders too obviously—though my eyes were about at stomach-level on him anyway. I was sure getting a good look at his abs. I could have built a house on a slab like that.

I could feel my face turn bright red. With my fair skin and dark hair, that wasn't really a good look for me.

"Mistress Rainey," he replied in his thick accent.

Oh, gosh, I could swear that his ultra-deep voice alone was going to make me swoon.

"Are you ready to go?" he asked. His accent made it sound like 'gae' not 'go'. For some reason that made me get all flustered and giggly again.

I took a deep breath. I didn't need to make a fool of myself. What would Starrie do?

I knew exactly what my twin sister would do in a situation like this.

I gave Drostan my biggest, most flirtatious smile. "I can't wait!" I threw in a bounce-and-clap for good measure.

Hopefully I wasn't pushing things too far. I wasn't exactly good at this flirting and talking to boys stuff. Starrie was the out-going one.

Even I admitted that I was more a follower than a leader. In fact, I was used to just coasting along doing whatever Starrie told me to do.

But Starrie wasn't here with me now. I was on my own.

With a super handsome stud of a centaur.

Drostan reached down for my hand. His own hand was about four times the size of my own and dwarfed me completely.

I'd never felt so small.

It's not like I was short or anything—my father was tall, and Starrie and I took after him more than we did my mom.

Since Drostan's hand took up all of my hand and about half of my arm, I ended up walking with my shoulder at an awkward angle, hurrying to take four steps for every one of his.

But I didn't really mind the discomfort. I was holding hands with a boy! Me!

For all her talk, I wasn't sure Starrie actually had ever held hands with someone. She couldn't have hidden something like that from me. I was pretty sure about that, anyway.

"Where are we going?" I asked, raising my voice to be heard above the clopping of his hooves on the cobblestones.

"There's going to be a bonfire by the beach," he answered in his deep, accented voice. "I thought it would be enjoyable."

"Fantastic." I felt a grin spread across my face from ear to ear. A bonfire on the beach with a handsome centaur. It was like something out of a book. I couldn't wait to see what the rest of the night held for us. Would I get to ride on his back? Would he introduce me to his other centaur friends—after all, I had promised Starrie that I would hook her up, hadn't I? I looked up at Drostan, wondering what it would be like to sit on his back and wrap my arms around him. Would he kiss me, I wondered.

I felt my face turn bright red. I was way jumping the gun on this one. Heck, we hadn't even officially started our first date yet. What was I doing thinking about kissing and all that stuff?

"Hussy," I muttered at myself.

"What's tha?" Drostan drawled, making me jump.

"Nothing," I said quickly, hoping he couldn't tell how red my face had turned. "I'm really excited you asked me to come with you."

A wide grin spread across his face. "Not nearly as excited as I am that you accepted," he said, giving my arm a little squeeze that nearly brought tears to my eyes. He was a lot stronger than he knew he was.

His words made me feel giddy and excited. I couldn't wait to get to the bonfire.

We didn't have far to go. We'd scarcely stepped onto the beach before I could hear the deep voices of the centaurs and the higher voices of humans surrounding the flickering light that was the bonfire. I bounced a few steps, eager to join them. I usually wasn't great about meeting new people, but being with Drostan had given my confidence a huge boost. I couldn't wait to be seen with him.

I looked around as we entered the circle of light surrounding the fire. There was a large group of about ten centaurs, with three other humans that I could make out sitting here at there among them. Two of the others were girls, but one was a guy who didn't look to be that much older than me. In fact, he looked familiar.

I wondered if he had gone to the same school as me. I'd been in and out of enough Magical schools that that was pretty likely. Starrie didn't like to stay put for too long, so we tended to get kicked out of schools pretty quickly.

Which was why our latest schooling was homeschooling. Mom had just figured it was better to cut her losses and stop spending so much time in the office with various principals hearing about our escapades.

If she'd liked that sort of thing, she would have stayed married to our dad. As it was, they'd only been married barely long enough for me and Starrie to announce our arrivals before they'd split—and Dad had been off to jail. Again. In fact, he pretty much spent more time in Magical holding facilities than he did out of them. He had a thing for mischief.

Starrie was like him like that.

What I could never figure out was why someone like Mom had married Dad in the first place. I mean, Dad was beyond charming when he wanted to be, but Mom was too smart to fall for something like that. There must have been some other reason for them to be together.

Drostan squeezed my hand/arm again and I lost my train of thought.

"Drostan," a chorus of voices shouted. "You made it! Look, you brought the girl!"

Drostan nodded. "Naturally I brought her."

Hoots and catcalls followed that remark.

I felt my eyebrows draw together. Something was starting to feel a little off about this date. Why were his centaur friends reacting in that way?

"She's cute," one of the centaurs said.

I felt my shoulders relax a little. That didn't sound quite as threatening.

"Here, sit," Drostan said, gesturing toward a log, next to the boy I had seen.

Of course the centaurs weren't sitting, but at least he had taken into consideration that I had smaller—and fewer—legs than he did.

"Um, hi," I said awkwardly to the boy who looked familiar.

"You're here with Drostan, then," he said, looking past me.

"Yeah," I said. "Who are you here with?"

He nodded his chin across the fire. "I'm supposedly here with Alpina, but I'm starting to get a bit of a weird vibe and was thinking about leaving." His eyes narrowed at me. "You don't recognize me, do you?"

I winced. "Sorry. I know you look familiar. I'm just really horrible with faces."

He shrugged. "That's OK. I wouldn't expect you to know who I am. I see you at the library all the time, though."

I tilted my head, something stirring in the back of my memory. "Of course, you're Chad! You work in the stacks in the library. I didn't recognize you without your glasses."

He pawed at his face as if just remembering that he wasn't wearing them.

"So you do remember me," his mouth widened in a grin.

"Does that mean you know who I am?" It wasn't really a fair game to play. Even my mom couldn't tell me and Starrie apart. Starrie and I had been to the library enough times together that he probably would have no idea which one I was.

"Of course I do," he said. "You're Wynter's youngest—Rainey."

Well, that got my attention. "You know my dad," I asked incredulously.

He shrugged, his brown hair picking up glints of red in the firelight. "I volunteer for the library at the prison. He talks about you and your sister a lot."

The first thought that came to my mind was rather snarky, so I decided not to answer at all.

"So, what brings you here with Alpina," I asked, instead.

He shrugged. "She asked me and I was curious enough to come. I don't know. Doesn't it seem a little off to you?"

I glanced over to where Drostan was talking with Chad's date, a gorgeously voluptuous centaur girl. I couldn't call how they were talking together anything else but flirting.

I shrugged.

Chad didn't get a chance to say anything more. Drostan noticed me looking at him and grinned, gesturing for me to go over to him. He grabbed me up and swung me up onto his back, just like in my daydream.

Only my daydream hadn't felt so public and so... awkward. I felt like I was marooned off in space somewhere. I'd ridden horses, but there was something formidable about the height I was seated at that made me feel like I might never be able to get down again.

I noticed that each of the other centaurs who had brought someone to the party had likewise thrown them onto their backs. Chad sat awkwardly on Alpina's back, looking as uncomfortable as I felt.

"Near on a thousand years ago," Drostan intoned, "humans came to our tribes. At first we lived in peace and harmony, but then a few of our men were accused of stealing the womenfolk from the human village."

My eyes met Chad's. I had a very bad feeling about all of this.

"The humans then took away our homes and scattered our tribes. So, today, we will follow the ancient traditions." He turned his face toward me and I shivered at the light gleaming there. It wasn't kind, it was proprietary. "I will make you mine, and you will serve me forever."

One of the other centaurs, one without a rider, trotted over to the bonfire, where he pulled something out of the flames.

It was an iron... a brand.

I thought I might faint.

I wasn't here on a date. I was being enslaved by a herd of centaurs.

Drostan dragged a heavy hand across my hair. "You'll love serving me, sweet," he murmured in my ear. "Your Magic will serve me well. This brand will bind you to me for a hundred years. The Magic is strong." He chuckled. "I knew when I saw you, that I had to make you mine."

I felt bile rise up in my throat.

I thought he might kiss me. I'd wanted him to, when the night had been young, but now the thought made me want to be sick. I thought I might do anything to have him back away from me.

"Rainey," I heard Chad call. I looked up at him, panic coloring my vision. He looked at me and raised both eyebrows.

He didn't say anything. I knew what he was asking me to do. I just knew.

And I knew that, if ever there was a time to call on that side of me, it was now.

Even if it scared me.

But I was Wynter Skye's daughter, which meant I was a descendent of the Morrigans. I had a legacy. It was a legacy I had been taught to avoid.

It might be enough to save us, if only I could pull myself together.

Trying to ignore Drostan's hot breath on my neck as he slid my hair to one side, no doubt so the branding iron could be pressed into the flesh in my shoulder, I closed my eyes and called the darkness to me. The darkness that was my birthright, my legacy, half of who I was.

Adrenaline pounded through my flesh. It felt like my heart was beating so fast that it was just one great humming sound instead of a thousand separate beats. Breathing ceased to exist. My Magic poured through me like a roaring river, tearing down everything in its way.

I didn't know if I could do this. The Magic was too strange, too new to me.

It was too strong. It frightened me.

How would I ever know, if I didn't try? Chad believed I could do it. For some reason I believed him. He knew my father, he knew what we Skyes were capable of.

He trusted me to be able to control it.

I opened my eyes and it was as dark as it had been with my eyes closed. I knew I still sat astride Drostan's back, but I could no longer feel the warmth of his coat or the harshness of his hands on my skin. All my senses were deadened, lost in the shadows I had drawn around us.

It couldn't last. I knew I wasn't strong enough to keep it together.

I gasped a little as I swung my legs together. I pulled a little of my Magic to myself, just enough for me to see what the others couldn't. Every being in the campfire circle was frozen in place, paralyzed by the darkness I had called. I was the only one moving, the only one aware.

I slid down from Drostan's back and ran across the sand, stumbling toward Alpina and Chad. Once my hand touched his skin, he jumped and looked down at me. His eyes found my unerringly, despite the darkness.

"You did this?" His voice was hushed.

I nodded. "We have to get the others. Quickly. I don't know how long I can sustain this." Already I could feel my Magic fraying at the edges. It was exhausting, trying to keep a group like this in paralysis for any stretch of time. I wasn't used to this kind of Magic. I didn't know how long I could handle it.

All I could think about was getting everyone to safety, so I could let the darkness go. I had to hang on long enough to see that through.

Together Chad and I found and awakened the girls that had been tricked by the centaurs. They were quick to grasp the situation and more than willing to escape while it was possible.

"Quickly," I urged, as we sprinted away from the fireside. "I can't hold it much longer."

The girls turned one way, while Chad grabbed my hand and we tore off in another.

I hoped he knew what he was doing.

Just as we fell back into a hollow in the sand, cushioned underneath a huge piece of hollowed driftwood, which arced like a roof above our heads, I felt the last of the dark trickle through my fingers.

"My sister will be looking for us," I warned. "Something like that, she won't be able to miss. She'll feel it. She always feels everything I do."

"Good," was all Chad said. "That was some serious Magic back there, Rainey. Your dad was right about you."

I wanted to answer, but the bellowing of angry centaurs filled the air. Unconsciously I scooted closer to Chad, taking comfort in his presence. I was grateful not to be alone.

Hoofs thundered past where we were hiding.

"They'll see our footprints," I whispered.

Chad shook his head. "No," he said. "I covered them. I'm an Air Witch."

Suddenly I was twice as grateful to be with him.

I cringed closer to him as more hooves surrounded the area. The centaurs weren't going to give up on finding us anytime soon. I just hoped that the other girls had managed to get away safely.

Chad slid an arm around me and cradled me closer. We slid a little deeper into the hollow under the log where the sand was cooler. I shivered a little and he rubbed my arms, his attention on the chaos around him.

"Protection charm," he murmured, when they passed us for the third time without looking under the log. "They'll never find us here. We just have to stay low."

He smelled nice, I realized, of pine wood smoke and something else, something warm and masculine. I pressed my back against his chest and let myself relax, trusting that he was as good as his word. We just had to wait.

Until Starrie found us.

Chad's hand rubbed up and down my arm. I was feeling a little warmer now, with the scent of him surrounding me. I was actually surprisingly comfortable, considering the strange turn my evening had taken.

"Rainey?" Chad whispered over my shoulder, his breath dancing through my hair.

"Yeah?" I turned partway in the darkness to look at him.

He leaned closer, his eyes on mine, and kissed me.

It was awful. First our noses collided, then, trying again, our chins. It was awkward and uncomfortable.

I started giggling and couldn't stop.

"Sorry," I whispered. I could pick up enough of Chad's emotions at this point to know that he was embarrassed. "Do you want to try that again?"

Surprise jolted through him. "Really?" he asked. "I mean, I know I'm no centaur..."

"No, but you make a really good hero," I answered. "You thought really fast out there, covered our bases, plus... you smell really nice." It was my turn to be glad of the covering of darkness, which hid the redness of my face. Had I really just told him I thought he smelled nice?

Was that even something a guy would want to hear from a girl?

Well, he had tried to kiss me, hadn't he?

I turned to face him properly and ran my fingers across his forehead and down one side of his face.

"You do want to kiss me, don't you?"

He nodded. In the darkness his eyes were a startling silvery gray. I wondered if he were part were. I wondered what his eyes would look like in the light. I had never really noticed.

My breath caught in my throat. Was this really me, in the dark with a boy I had only just met, asking him if he wanted to kiss me?

I knew what Starrie would say if she were here with me. Live a little, that's what she would say.

Chad's fingers played with my hair as we looked at each other, eye to eye, breathing in the same air. He looked at my mouth and I closed my eyes.

His lips brushed mine. Once, twice, then more firmly. His arm slid down from my shoulders to around my waist. He pulled me against him and kissed me again, deeper this time.

Warmth filled me. I forgot we were hiding in a hole in the ground. I forgot that I was supposed to be on a date with a centaur. All I could remember was that I was here with

Chad—the quiet boy from the library who had known that I was Rainey, Wynter's daughter. Who had known that I could call on the right Magic to save us.

I could feel him staring at me in the darkness. I opened my eyes. His heart stammered under my hand. His eyes, what I could see of them, had turned to liquid silver.

Holy and ancient things, he was beautiful. How had I missed that? How could I never have noticed what was right in front of my eyes.

"I knew it," he whispered against my lips, "I knew you were special."

This time I was the one that kissed him.

For once, I didn't care if Starrie could feel what I was feeling. This once, I felt like it was just me—me and Chad.

It was dawn when my sister found us, nestled together like twin rabbits in a burrow.

"Hmm," she said, as we headed back toward our waiting families and the million questions that waited for us. She stared at Chad over her shoulder, as if he needed her stamp of approval. "Not a centaur, but not bad, Little Sis. He's cute, in a kind of nerdy way."

I grinned to myself. Let Starrie have her few minutes of seniority. Let her feel superior and patronizing. For once, I didn't care.

I looked over my shoulder at Chad. His eyes met mine. In the daylight they were a soft gray, the same exact shade as the early morning fog on the ocean beside us. A grin spread across his face. His white teeth glinted in his tan face.

I wondered what kind of were blood he had running through his veins. I'd have to find out later.

We didn't need to say anything to each other. I knew I would see him later. It was a sure thing, as sure as I was Wynter Skye's daughter, as sure as I had called the darkness to me and used it to escape. I would see him soon. I knew it without a doubt.

In the meantime, I had a feeling I was going to be grounded for the rest of my life for sneaking out to be with a centaur and spending the night with a strange boy. My mother was going to flip out and throw the book at me—maybe a hundred books, if the expression on her face was any indication.

"Worth it," I murmured, my mouth turning up at the corners triumphantly.

"Boy," Starrie murmured. "You have a lot to tell me when we get home."

I smiled at her. Let her think I was going to tell her all.

I was going to keep Chad and his liquid silver eyes and warm kisses to myself. She might think she could feel it all, but Chad... Chad was mine.

I reached Mom's side. She had her arms folded around herself and that look on her face that suggested that one word—any word—out of my mouth and she was going to send me to the worst witch boarding school on the planet.

I caught Chad's eye again, across the sand. He stood with a tall man and woman that had to be his parents, as well as a few official-looking people.

"They want a statement," my mother said, as if they were asking for one of my arms, instead of something reasonable. "I don't know what you've gotten yourself into, Rainey. If it were Starrie..."

"Sorry, Mom," I said automatically. "I was wrong. I snuck out to go on a date with a centaur and he tried to make me his slave. Believe me, I think I've learned my lesson. I'll take any punishment you see fit to give me, though. I know I've earned it."

Her mouth flapped open and shut a few times. "You girls," she said with an air of helplessness, "are going to drive me crazy."

Starrie and I grinned at each other. It wasn't every day we could get a confession like that out of our unflappable mother.

It felt an awful lot like a win to me.

I lifted an arm and waved at Chad as he turned to follow his parents off of the beach. He immediately turned his head and waved back at me.

"Maybe Mom will ground me to the library for life," I said.

Starrie groaned and rolled her eyes. "Seriously, Rainey. You have an adventure like this and all you can think about is going to the library? Sometimes I despair for you."

"Hey," I said, smiling a secret smile to myself. "I like the library. You meet all kinds of interesting people there."

Summer in Summerland

I feel sorry for the girl in my class who has the disadvantage of being a were spider. If the Fates were real it was super unfair of them to saddle her with something like that. I mean, even the were squirrel in our class had a chance at having a decent experience in our Magical high school.

But a were spider? Not a chance.

OK, so Arana was a little strange to begin with. A spider girl should have been Goth at least, or maybe just a little bit dark and creepy.

But in her human form Arana was a small, insipid-looking washed out blond with a button nose and equally washed out blue eyes. The only spider-y thing about her were her super long fingers, which tapped nervously on her desk. Her desk was right across the aisle from mine and the light staccato was starting to make me feel a little crazy. Did she always have to tap like that? All class, every class, it was tap. Tap. Tap. Over and over again.

"Miranda Duncan," Miss Jessup said, snapping me out of my annoyed little reverie. I figuratively leapt to attention at the sound of her voice. "Can you please explain the Creed of Magic and why it is so important?"

I shot a last look at Arana's tapping fingers and settled myself into answering the question.

"The Creed of Magic states," I said evenly. "the three laws of Magic. One—every act of Magic creates a consequence. This is called the Ripple law. It states that if a were butterfly flaps its wings in Peru at the wrong moment the entire world could collapse. Thus the Magic practitioner must always be aware and practice only 'white' or 'clean' Magics—those with measurably safe levels of impact on the world.

"Two—Magic comes in many forms. There are Magical beings—such as born weres, not bitten, selkie, and other non-elemental persons. Then there are elemental beings— the nymphs, dryads, undines, fire-pixies, gnomes and such. Then there are Magical Practitioners—those born with power reflecting one of the elements. Once there were Fae, but they have been separate from us for centuries. According to the Creed, each of these groups contributes an equal and essential part of balance in Magic.

"The third law states that Magic unused will always seek the easiest point of escape. Because of this all Magical being must use their powers regularly and wisely to avoid problems.

"The fourth law applied to when Faerie was still part of our world. The Creed states that no one shall ever have contact with Faerie. Ever."

Miss Jessup nodded, accepting my answer, though I knew that I'd been a little sloppy.

"Do no harm," she said smoothly, ticking the laws off on her fingers. "All are equal in Magic. Use, or be used. Stay away from Faerie."

We chanted the words with her, as we did at the end of every school day.

Geez, I thought, we've got it already!

She dismissed us and I grabbed up my books. I was one of the first out of the door.

"Have a good summer vacation," I heard Miss Jessup shout from behind us.

I rolled my eyes. I knew exactly what kind of summer vacation I was going to be facing. My mother had me signed up for so many camps and 'opportunities' that I wasn't even going to have time to take a breath for the next three months.

I was so busy grounding my teeth that I nearly ran Arana over. I mean, she was standing right there. How could I have missed seeing her?

It was like she tried to be invisible.

Arana turned and stared at me, her pale blue eyes taking on a weird vacant expression. I felt a fist of ice clamp over my spine. I had known Arana long enough to know that she was having one of her 'visions'.

"What do you see?" I asked, softly, knowing that it was the right thing to do. In truth, I had no interest in hearing what Arana had to say. I wanted to get out of the doors and a few hours of freedom before my wings were clipped, yet again, by my mother and all her plans for me.

Arana's long fingers stretched toward me. I braced myself, ready to turn and run if she actually tried to touch me.

"You," she intoned, in a strangely deep voice, "will find the love of your life this summer. It will change you, and it will change two worlds."

She straightened abruptly and blinked, her insipid eyes clearing. "Oh," she said in her usual, tiny voice. "Am I blocking you? I'm sorry, Miranda."

"It's OK, Arana," I managed. "Have a good summer."

She waved her fingers over her shoulders as she trotted off, completely oblivious to the blow she had delivered me.

Find the love of my life this summer? Right, like that was ever going to happen. That was the one thing that was guaranteed never to happen in my lifetime.

I was a Duncan woman. We never found love. Happily Ever After didn't exist in our line.

Heck, there hadn't been a man strong or stubborn enough to stick around a Duncan woman since we were huddled around peat-fires cursing people like the good Scottish witches we were.

My own father hadn't even stuck around long enough to know that my mom was pregnant with me. I didn't know much about him. I really didn't need to know much, either. I was Duncan through and through. Like all Duncan women I had pale skin, maybe a shade darker than new snow, with dark mahogany hair, dark black eyes, and rose red lips.

After all, we were the most powerful Magical family of all. Descended from the original Snow White, if my mother was to be believed.

I looked the part.

My 'father' had been from Mongolia. My only legacy from him was the almond shape of my eyes and an extra dose of deep Earth Magic heaped on top of the Duncan legacy.

From the time I'd been six I'd known I was the strongest Earth Witch of my generation. Everybody knew it. In fact, I'd been so strong when I was little that my mother and grandmother had had to bind my powers until I could stop causing earthquakes every time I had a temper tantrum. That alone was something of a miracle. It had to be the only thing my mother and grandmother had willingly done together since my mother was my age.

I shook my head. Arana might be the voice piece of the Fates, but there was no way her vision about me would ever come true.

I was doomed and destined to be alone for my entire life. Duncan women were always alone. Just like Duncan women never had sons, just daughters.

Legend had it, if a Duncan woman ever had a son, the curse would be broken and she would be with her love forever.

That's how desperate the women in my family had gotten. We just all wanted to believe that there could be someone out there for us—somewhere.

I opened my locker and dumped the entire contents into my bag. I wasn't going to miss this place. Heck, I didn't even intend to attend my graduation. I had three days of freedom before I'd be shipped off the first of many camps my mother had signed me up for. Let her worry about graduation. I was out.

I patted my purse and smiled.

I had some plans of my own to take care of.

For a Magical practitioner as strong as me, it was simple enough to take one of the practice chariots from the school and re-spell it for a new location. Sure, I could have taken the bus, at least part-way, but what was the fun in that?

I was rebelling. I was supposed to be a little reckless, right?

I wasn't sure. I'd never really rebelled before.

I'd always just done exactly what Mother wanted me to do. I'd followed with her plans, down to every dotted 'i' and every crossed 't'.

But I was starting to realize that it was never going to end. I couldn't live my entire life to please my mother. For one thing, she was never ever going to be pleased with me. There would always be something else to reach for, something else I needed improvement on. No matter what I did, I was never going to be enough for her.

For another—what about me? I was seventeen years old and still hadn't managed to assert the fact that I hate, loathed, despised, green beans and pancakes. Was it a life or death kind of deal? No. But if I wasn't even allowed to choose what foods I liked or hated... Well, this rebellion had been a long time coming.

In fact, I'd been planning some version of this escape since I was eight years old and my mother had decided, for both of us, that I was going to give up competing on horses and focus on my Magic. Off she had sent my pony, Faustus, telling me that I couldn't always get my way.

Even then I was sick of all the can'ts in my life. "You can't have friends over, you need to focus on your Magic. You're a Duncan woman, after all," or, "You can't go there with your friends, you're a Duncan", "You can't wear that", "You can't do that", "You can't go to that party".

Can't. Can't. Can't.

Well, just let them wait and see.

Because I was going to break the biggest, baddest, can't of them all.

I was going to break into Faerie.

No one was going to tell me what I could and couldn't do ever again.

My first stop was to the Middle Lands—the midpoint between the 'mortal' world and the barrier between us and Faerie. It was there that I knew I was going to have to pull out the big guns.

In this case, my family tree.

"I need a two-way ticket in and out of Faerie," I told the King and Queen, giving them my sweetest smile, the one that made the dimple next to my mouth pop out. I practically oozed charm. That was one thing I had learned from my mother all these years.

The Queen was sitting next to her husband, a chunky toddler with golden curls sitting on her lap.

The situation couldn't have been more perfect for my needs.

"I'm a Duncan," I said, knowing that the family's reputation preceded me. Everyone knew about the Duncans. "I know what the price is, and I'm willing to pay it."

"Your oldest daughter will marry our son?" The King glanced at the little boy on his wife's knee as I nodded.

I had no intention of ever having a daughter, though I wasn't about to tell these kind people that. I wasn't even planning on having kids, but if I was going to, I was pretty sure I had enough Earth Magic to work around the Duncan curse and make sure I only had boys.

They knew it was a good trade. My family had power in spades, and it helped that we tended to be way above average in the looks department too. I wasn't being prideful about that—it just was true. Even my mother—who had gone gray as a teenager—was gorgeous enough that would-be suitors were almost literally popping out of the plentiful woodwork around our cottage.

So, I found myself with my ticket into Faerie. All it had cost was the hand of my eldest daughter in marriage.

Everything was working out according to plan.

The spell the royal family gave me, augmented with my own resources, had enough power to propel me straight past the barrier, the Wild Magic that supported it, and into the heart of Faerie.

I ignored the looks of concern on the faces of the royal family. Now that they had given me what I wanted, they were having doubts.

"Faerie is blocked away from us for a reason," the queen said uneasily. "It is not the place for a young child like you."

I just smiled at her. What was she going to do, now that the bargain had been made? She couldn't forcibly take the spells from me, and I had no intention of backing away now.

One more step, and I would be out of the reach of my mother and everyone else in my world. I would show them what I could do—let the rules be damned.

Faerie didn't frighten me. I knew my Magic would keep me safe.

I knew if I didn't go now, I would regret it for the rest of my life. It would be like consenting to be my mother's puppet forever. If I walked away, I knew I would never truly get to be myself. I would just yield and yield until there was nothing of Miranda left to fight.

And I was done with that.

"Thank you," I called, as I activated the first spell—the one that would take me into Faerie. The other would wait until I was ready to come home—if I ever was.

The world shifted around me. The earth rumbled underneath my feet.

And, suddenly, I was... elsewhere.

Faerie.

There are things that all forests have in common, and Faerie was no different. Those were the things I first noticed—the birdsong, the shimmer of sunlight drifting down through tree boughs. The whisper of tiny things, pushing through the mulch to grow straight and tall—all these were as familiar to me as my reflection in the quiet pool at my feet.

But it was those similarities that made the differences so... abrupt.

There were trees I recognized, of course, but for every oak and elm there were trees I had no names for—some silvery and slender, like birches, but actually silver, not just silver in color. Some had drooping branches like the willows at home, but were dotted with crimson flowers that we all-too reminiscent of drops of blood.

The air was thick with unfamiliar scents. The dampness of the earth itself should have smelled familiar to me, with all the hours I'd spent digging around in the soil in my lifetime. But it wasn't familiar, it was rich and loamy and the scent was wild, full of promise.

Full of Magic.

Oh, the Magic was thick in the air. It was heavy and abundant in the Earth, in the roots, in the plants themselves. Everywhere I turned there was Magic surrounding me. It tingled through my skin. It danced through my veins and curled through the ends of my hair. It made me want to sing and dance and shout and run.

Me. Miranda. I never did that sort of thing. I'd never even felt the slightest urge to break randomly into song and dance like all those people in musicals. I was just not that kind of girl.

Faerie made me want to rethink that part of myself.

I felt so free.

It suddenly struck me that here I was, beyond the reach of any person I had ever known. I'd done it. I had walked away from convention and law and gone in my own direction. If I wanted to, I could stay here forever. No one would ever make me leave, if I didn't want to.

My mother couldn't reach me here. She couldn't control me.

I was truly free.

I had no idea what to do with myself.

I was here. I was in the middle of Faerie, and I was at loose ends for the first time in my life. I had planned so long and so hard how I was going to get here that I had not even considered what I would do once I was actually here.

For one thing, the practical side of me warned, I had nowhere to sleep once nighttime came. I knew enough about history to know that not everything inside the borders of Faerie were benign. In fact, even the beings considered 'good' of the Fae were often deadly and dangerous to mortals.

"Right," I said out loud. My voice sounded strange. All the birds in the area hushed at the sound. "I've got to find a place to camp for the night. And I suppose I should try to find something to eat while I'm at it."

At least I had my Magic. It was a simple matter to send a tendril of power into the earth and send out feelers—food, I requested, shelter, safety.

If people had roots, this is what it would feel like. Some fingers of my Magic warned me about going in those directions. What might be there, I had no idea, but I knew that it didn't 'feel' right.

A couple others sent back signals that there was food and shelter in those directions.

I followed the strongest of these tingles. I assumed that the stronger tug would be from someplace closer than the others.

Well, if I was wrong, there were plenty of other feelers out for promising locations. The sun was still high up, I had plenty of time.

I blinked as I realized that, based on the shadows of the leaves of the trees, it was apparently earlier in the day here than it had been in the Middle Lands when I'd left.

I'd heard that time was different in Faerie. Now I was seeing it first-hand.

As far as I knew, I'd already been away from home for a hundred years.

Maybe the thought of that should have made me feel sad, but it didn't, not really.

Was it wrong of me to resent my mother so much that being out of her reach felt like being handed a whole new universe? I knew I was being an ungrateful and horrible child.

And I still didn't care.

There. That was the truth. The real Miranda was a cold, unfeeling, horrible person. Because the real Miranda wasn't grateful for what she'd been given, she was just relieved to escape.

I felt like singing, but I didn't know what song to sing, so I just traipsed along the path that my Magic was pulling me along. I didn't skip—not quite.

I felt a strange buzzing in the air. If calling my Magic made the air tingle, this felt like an entire thunderstorm of Magic—perhaps a full-on hurricane of a storm of Magic.

I barely had time to duck behind a tree before the clearing I'd just departed was consumed with golden fire.

It came so suddenly that it could have been lightning, but I'd never seen lightning like this. It burned, but there was no heat, just a heavy weight in the air like something momentous was about to occur.

The flash of light vanished and there stood a form. I thought for a moment that it had wings, or that it was made of the light itself, but then the brightness faded and left a man standing before me.

I'd never seen a man like this. His skin was fair, with an almost silvery cast to it. Part of my mind realized that I was seeing only a fraction of what he was. Was he some kind of god? An angel?

The last rays of the light he had generated kissed his true-red hair as he turned toward me. His eyes unerringly found me, though I'd thought myself well hidden behind my chosen tree.

His eyes were a compelling shade of gray. I found myself stepping towards him, my feet moving of their own volition. I wondered, in the back of my mind, if I was stepping towards my doom, but the rest of me just didn't care.

He was beautiful. He was glorious. He was perfection. And not one of those words could begin to convey even a single line of his face.

There was nothing human or mortal about him.

"You," he said, in a voice as grandiose as the rest of him, "are a stranger here."

I managed to nod. My mouth was too dry to even try to form words. I dragged my hands through my hair, hoping that I didn't look too much like I'd just crossed earth, the Middle Lands, and the barrier just to be here.

He stepped closer. Geez, whatever he was, they certainly didn't believe in personal space. He stood so closely to me that I could feel heat pouring off of his body. It warmed me right to my toes.

It also made me feel a little light-headed.

What was that scent around him? It was something so unique, so exotic, and yet tantalizingly familiar.

He smelled like Home.

My inner self scoffed at the thought, the instant it leapt up into my brain, but it refused to be cowed.

He's the one, my brain screamed in rapture, he's your forever love! Here's your Faerie Tale standing right in front of you.

His eyes were watching my face as who knew what expressions flew across the surface. His breath stirred the hair on the nape of my neck.

I wanted to step away. I wanted to step closer.

I wanted him to do something. Because him standing still like that was killing me.

I knew he was taking it all in—the shaking of my hands, the gasping of my breath. His eyes wandered over my face again, before settling on my eyes.

"Who are you," he asked. There was no challenge in the words. His voice, if anything, sounded like he was marveling to see something different—someone new—in front of him.

"I'm Miranda Duncan," I announced, drawing my shoulders back with every ounce of the hereditary pride that name bestowed. I lifted my chin, meeting his silvery gaze as unflinchingly as I could considering the fact that my inner mind was set on having a romantic tizzy screaming things like 'fate' and 'destiny' and 'oh, my gosh, he's so cute'!

Obviously my internal dialogue needed to get out more.

"I don't know you." Again, the words were filled with wonder.

I shook back my hair and clasped my hands together to keep myself from gnawing my fingernails off. Did he have to stare at me quite like that? So intensely?

"No," I said. "I'm not from here. I'm... from the other side of the barrier."

His reaction was immediate. He stepped back. Shock, anger, concern—they all crossed his face in a matter of moments.

"We need to get you someplace safe," he said urgently. "If I sensed you, they will too. You are not safe here. You should not be here."

He grabbed my arm.

Heat so intense it should have incinerated me into a thousand cinders scorched through my skin, down through my bones. Flames danced up around my eyes. My ears roared with thunder.

The clearing vanished.

I found myself in a stone room of some kind, filled with books and a roaring fireplace. The only windows were too high for me to look out, but they had a gothic shape to them, making me wonder if we weren't in the tower of an actual castle.

I turned to the man—the being—beside me. If this was a castle, would that make him a prince?

My prince?

Shut up, I told that little voice inside of me.

"You will be safe here," he said. For the first time I realized that his words had a strange accent. I supposed that I'd been distracted by his rather celestial appearance so much that I had not noticed that whatever language he was speaking didn't fall naturally on my ears.

I had a hunch neither of us was speaking English anymore.

"You will be guarded by my Magic," he was saying. "None will be able to find you."

"Um," I managed. "Thanks? But, you know, my mother told me never to talk to strangers let alone go home with them, so I think I'll take a ride back down to the woods, if you don't mind."

No! Shrieked my internal voice. You idiot! What are you doing? Don't you want to be alone with his royal hottiness?

I had to keep myself from rolling my eyes at myself. Seriously.

"No," he said, folding his arms over his chest. "I cannot allow that."

I felt my eyebrows attempt to jump off of my forehead in shock. "I'm sorry, what? You can't *allow*? Who died and made you King of the universe?"

His forehead drew down in puzzlement. After a moment it cleared.

"My father," he said.

"Oh crap," I breathed, stepping back away from him. "You're the King?"

He raised his chin. "I'm the Seraphim of Faerie. I am Lenus."

"Look Mr. Lenus, or whatever you go by, are you saying you're not going to let me go?"

He shook his head. "Not until I can be sure you will be safe. Your kind is not looked upon kindly here."

Yeah, I'd kind of gotten that impression when he'd said I wasn't safe.

He stood there silently, staring at me for so long that I started to feel like a museum exhibit or a pen at the zoo or something.

"What?" I finally demanded, just to break the silence. "What is it?"

He tilted his head, considering the question more seriously than it merited.

"It's you," he said finally. "There's something about you. You're different... you're mortal.... But there is something else."

He reached out a hand and brushed the tips of his fingers against my cheek.

His touch was searing, yet not unpleasant. It was like being touched by a ray of sunlight on a cold day. It did funny things to the pit of my stomach.

Glory hallelujah, my inner voice rejoiced.

Our eyes met, and the next thing I knew we were kissing.

I wasn't sure, precisely, who had kissed who. Had he made the first move? Had I? Had we somehow met in the middle?

It felt an awful lot like simple combustion.

And, boy was I burning up.

Maybe Arana was right. Maybe the Fates had decreed this—all of this.

But I knew one thing, that instant when our lips met for the first time.

I would never love anyone as much as Lenus, should I live to be a thousand years old.

I was equally sure that this love—this forbidden kiss— would change both of our worlds, forever.

D' Jinn Big Trouble

It's cliché by now, that whole 'Be careful what you wish for' deal. I know that—I grew up with it. My parents harped on that enough when I was a kid that you would think that the mantra would have saturated my brain waves—or at least prepared me for facing any situation in which wishing was warranted.

Sadly, that was not the case.

"This is all your fault," I hissed to my companion.

He just smiled contentedly, not even bothering to answer.

We both knew whose fault it was that we were in this situation.

That would be me.

It all started when I was off working on the Food Truck for the bakery that me and my girlfriends, Cindy and Tansy, had recently opened. It fell on me because Tansy was having some kind of meltdown and Cindy was caught up in yet another Magical mess.

We were all feeling a little giddy. We were overworked, for sure.

And I was under the influence of a Love spell gone awry. I mean, I mention that because it's only fair. I know that now, but I didn't then. I just don't want anyone assuming that I usually behave in such a rash, wild way.

So, when the hottie-mocha-latte, as my girlfriends would have teased me, showed up in line for some of our specialty chocolate toads—not real toads, no worries there, our food is awesome—I started to flirt with him.

I mean, come on. Any girl would have done the same.

He had this white smile in his dark-yet-golden face and the world's baldest head. On him, it looked nice. I mean, I like a guy with hair, but just seeing this guy made me start rethinking my ideas of what made a guy attractive and what didn't.

Though I was pretty much equal-opportunity with my dating, this guy... well, my reaction to him suggested that I suddenly had a type.

So, we flirted while I bagged up his order and he kept flashing those white teeth and dimples at me.

And he said something along the lines of, "Wow, it's so busy. How do you keep up, Magic?"

And I said, and this is a direct quote, "I only wish I had Magic."

Bam. Boom. POW!

My life turned upside down just like that.

How the hell was I supposed to know that I'd been flirting with a genie?

Only, get this, they loathe that word. No, no—they go by 'D'jinn'. And this whole three wishes business? Nope, that's not a thing either.

No, next thing I know Mr. Hottie is announcing he's my friendly neighborhood D'jinn... forever.

And, even worse, I am his new apprentice.

OK, so my roommate and bestie, Cindy—she's the one who is into Magic. I mean, she's actually Magical. I'd just gotten used to that.

But I was in no way looking to be hitching a ride on the Magical express. I liked my life just fine, thank you. I had the bakery, I had my friends... sure, I liked to flirt a little, but that was all part of the fun and games of being a young, attractive woman, right?

So my reaction to all this news?

And I quote: "Oh, hell no."

Alecto was gorgeous, but I was not throwing myself into a permanent relationship based on exactly thirty seconds of flirting and one unfortunate choice of words.

"That's entrapment," I hissed at him. "You can't just walk in here and change my life. You made me say that."

He grinned that super-smooth grin at me and shook his head. "Nope. That was all you."

I thought he might be about to say something about it being Fate, so I decided to interrupt him. "This is not happening," I told him. "I don't care what the rules are—you'd better turn around and walk away if you know what's best for you."

He shrugged. "I can't. Now that you're an official D'jinn in training, you have to be under surveillance twenty-four seven. Unless, of course, you wanted me to call in some of the other D'jinn?"

Something in his voice suggested that was a very bad idea.

"I'll tell you what," I told him. "I'm going to call my friend's stepdad and see if you're playing me straight."

He raised an eyebrow.

"Oh, you'd better watch out," I said. "He's on the Western Council of Magic and he's not known for messing around." Of course, I didn't know if Stephan was actually like that, but I could use a little bluster and padding on my side.

I wanted this D'jinn to be shaking in his—I checked his feet—flip-flops?

OK, he obviously needed my fashion help.

Talking to Stephan Marcellus only told me what Alecto was saying was the truth.

"Don't tell anyone," he warned. "Until you are fully trained, you will be extremely vulnerable. Don't even tell Cindy. I'm going to do my best to forget that I ever heard any of this."

Nice.

And I was on my own again.

I fought the urge to call my parents.

Not that I didn't think they would believe me—my dad's Irish through and through and my mom is from Trinidad—both were full enough of superstitions to accept things like Magic without hesitation.

Only, I'd promised never to tell anyone about Magic.

That, and Stephan had pretty much just told me that telling my parents about my new little problem would put them into danger.

That was so not going to happen.

Argh.

People suck.

"You," I said, stabbing my finger at Alecto's chest, "are on my bad side. You step out of line and I am going to make you wish you'd never come out of your bottle."

"Actually," he said, "that's a myth too."

"Well, then," I said, sweetly. "You're going to wish you had a bottle."

His grin only widened. "I guess, then, it's a bad time to ask you out?"

I sighed and rolled my eyes. "Fine. I need a date for this wedding I'm going to anyway."

I can practically hear you shaking your head at me, wondering what all the fuss is about.

I'll tell you what—now I'm dating a guy I can't ever get away from, I'm training with Magic that isn't even considered to be good-guy Magic, I can't tell anyone about any of this...

And the sonuvagun just stole the last chocolate toad on the truck.

That damn D'jinn's in big trouble when I catch him.

Avow

Ethan Tanner sat in his car, staring blankly out of the windshield.

He didn't pay any attention to his surroundings, he just sat, listening to his mind go around and around without stopping.

Ethan dropped his head in his hands, his fingers tugging at his thick, wiry, blond hair. His finger dug deeper, brushing against his scalp. He sat up, looking into the rear-view mirror, trying to see anything weird, anything wrong at all.

From the outside he looked perfect, like any other healthy twenty year old with a full life ahead of him. College, marriage, a family, everything that a child bounced from one foster home to another his whole life craved, all of that should have been in his future.

"One year," Ethan whispered. "One year."

He closed his eyes against the overwhelming flood of hopelessness.

He couldn't believe it. Even though the doctors had shown him images of the mass that was growing virulently in his brain, he could not comprehend what was happening to him.

"Do you have a family history of brain tumors?" He'd been asked.

"I don't know," Was all he could answer. How could he explain that he had been dumped off outside of a grocery store at the ripe age of three, clutching an ice cream cone and screaming for his mother? "I don't have any family history."

Ethan struck out at the steering wheel, jumping when it beeped in protest.

"I have no family," he muttered. "I have no family and now I am going to die. I am alone and I'm going to die."

His throat tightened, burning with suppressed tears.

He fumbled with the lock on his car door and stumbled out. A gust of wind off of the beach beat against him, heavy with the promise of rain. Ethan threw his head back, drinking in the salty smell that permeated the air around him.

"No wonder they used to send terminal cases to the seaside," he thought, wryly.

He shucked off of his shoes, striding across the deep sands of the beach.

The waves roared at him, white-capped and violent, whipped up by the wind.

"I should just end it," Ethan whispered. "If I'm going to die anyway, I might as well go now, at my own hand. I could just walk out there, into the sea... and drift away."

The rock in his chest burned furiously. He rubbed at it, swallowing hard.

He couldn't do it. He wanted to live.

"Help me," he whispered. He didn't even know who he was asking. He didn't know if he believed in God, or if God was the one who wanted him to die. He just knew he couldn't face this impossible road alone. "Please," he roared, over the crashing of the waves. "Please, help me!"

"Please," he chanted, his voice full of terrible need. "I want to live. I haven't even lived. I want a wife and a family and to see my children grow up..."

The sea, the sand, the wind, the seal sunning itself on the rocks, all became his confessors. He poured his soul out to them.

"I've never even known love," he said, bitterly. "All I have wanted is to be loved, to find and give what I never had as a child."

His head throbbed violently. He clutched at it. "Please," he whispered desperately. "Won't anyone help me?"

The storm hushes abruptly. Ethan's gaze was drawn back towards the water, the waves calmed and still.

The rock in his chest turned into the flittering of a butterfly.

A pair of liquid brown eyes stared out at him from the water. It was a seal.

No, it was a girl. She stood up in the water slowly, her eyes on his. There was something strange a beautiful about those eyes. Ethan couldn't breathe.

Her dark hair, dripping down her back, was long and dark. She wore a simple white shift that clung to her, sodden. Her face had an unearthly beauty to it, pale and perfect with those large, liquid, brown eyes.

Tears rolled silently down her face as she waded towards him.

She stopped, standing in front of him, gazing unwaveringly into his eyes. She reached out a small, white hand to touch his arm.

Ethan jolted at the touch. She was real.

"I could love you," she said.

Her voice was accented, strange to his ears. Like her appearance, there was an otherworldly quality about it. It was rich and soft, soothing.

"What?" Ethan gasped. Her hand on his arm sent warmth through him. It was comforting. He wanted to wrap himself up in it.

"I would love you like that," she said, still gazing up at him with compassion, and something else.

"How? What?" Ethan couldn't draw his thoughts together.

"You called me," she murmured. "You called me to you because you need me."

"I'm dying," Ethan said, bluntly.

"I know," she said. "You're dying and you've never been loved. You want a family. You want to live. I can give you that."

Ethan swallowed. "Who... what are you?"

She smiled, softly, lighting up her already angelic face. "I'm Eithne. I am selkie."

Ethan shook his head, doubt filling his whole being. He ran his hands through his hair. Was this all a hallucination brought on by the brain tumor?

But he had seen her rise from the sea.

In his heart he knew it was true.

He needed it to be true.

"Can you help me?" His voice broke from the force of the ray of hope that shot through him.

She nodded, her heavy hair curling around her face. "Yes," she breathed.

She leaned closer to him. He could smell the sea on her, something wild, and sweet. She pressed her cheek against his chest.

Warmth flowed through his whole body. He clung to her.

He saw them walking side by side, hand-in-hand, smiling at each other, a golden ring around her finger.

He saw her sitting at his knee as he stroked her dark hair, her belly full and round.

He saw them, together, in a little cottage by the sea, his arms around her as they looked down at their precious little one.

He saw himself, an older man, lying still in a hospital bed. A beautiful young woman stood beside him, her fingers laced through his. She had curly long hair and his eyes.

"Dad," she whispered.

Ethan's eyes opened. He looked down at the little selkie, who had left the sea, answering his call.

She nodded again, her face serene. "I can give you that. All of that. All that you asked: Love, a family, a child..."

"And I won't die?" He managed to whisper.

"Not yet," she answered. "Someday you will, but not yet."

He bent his head to bury his nose in her hair. Tears, the first he had shed, welled up in his eyes and slid down his face, resting in her hair like tiny pearls.

He could not speak the words to beg her to stay, to fulfill all she offered him. He could not express himself, for the hope that made him weep.

She looked up at him, her face aglow with love, with promise.

"I promise," she whispered.

Baehrly Beginning

Chapter One

"Well," I said out loud to nobody in particular, "it's a lovely day here in Siberia."

There was no answer, but I wasn't really expecting one.

I was standing in the middle of nowhere. Literally. My map actually called this place 'Nowhere'. Of course, the map, a gift from my deceased father, did have an exhaustive sense of humor. Or was it exhausting? I could never be quite sure.

"Cute," I growled at it, giving it a shake before stuffing it into my pack. It was going to give me hell later for treating it like that—it insisted on being folded properly—but I had more important things on my mind than trying to figure out finicky accordion folds.

I'd been trying to track down the leak of miniature mastodon relics into the Magical black market for months. Ivory, wool, bones, teeth—they all had been appearing at a reckless pace considering that the species was almost completely extinct.

"Freakin' idiots," I muttered as I pulled on a pair of mittens from my pack. It was freezing out here. Wasn't it supposed to be summer?

Apparently someone forgot to send Siberia the memo.

Good thing I was always prepared.

I patted my hip to make sure my sword belt was still in place after being transported around the globe in seconds. I always half-expected to leave something behind.

Just as I was about to set off into the wilderness my pack let out a truly obnoxious sound. It was something between a foghorn blast and the shriek of steel that usually marks the demise of a vehicle via crashing into a tree.

It was also unfortunately familiar.

"Fred," I scolded, as I yanked my bag off of my back again and opened it up.

My zombie silkie rooster blinked up at me with his obscene red eyes.

"What are you doing here?" I demanded, dumping him out with little ceremony into the cold ground. It couldn't hurt him. After all, he was already dead.

Once, Fred had been someone's cute and fuzzy pet silkie, silkies being the lapdog of the chicken world. That is, until he had been hit by a truck. Some wiseass had decided the best thing to do at that point was to reanimate him.

Little cute zombies could be a pain in the butt.

Of course, it was *my* job to take care of Fred and keep him out of trouble, which is why he was supposed to be at home being watched by my sister at this moment.

I was seriously tempted to take Fred back home then and there. I would have, too, only transportation spells tended to make me feel sick to my stomach, and the further I traveled the worse the sickness was.

It just wasn't worth it.

I tucked Fred under my arm. I couldn't expect him to hike, after all.

"You're becoming a vegetarian when we get home," I told him seriously. "How about an all onion diet?"

Fred cocked his head and gave me some serious stink-eye. Even the idea of onions got his feathers in a bunch.

"Last time I ask Iris to keep an eye on you!" I muttered to my chicken. I frowned. "Though I wouldn't put it past her to have stuffed you in my bag herself just for that reason."

Fred blinked at me.

I sighed. "So, maybe it's Iris that needs some onions."

Fred preened his feathers.

Ugh. I was having a conversation with a chicken and, unlike my twin sisters, Starrie and Rainey Skye, I couldn't understand what he might be saying back.

Maybe that was a good thing.

I didn't really need to know what my zombie rooster thought of me.

The terrain grew rougher as I headed up the track the map had marked as 'deeper into nowhere' in its usual helpful manner. I muttered a brief spell, one that was pretty much just a plea to the earth to stay under my feet.

Immediately I felt a little sturdier.

I was nowhere as powerful as my mother, the most powerful Earth witch of her generation, but I was a pretty good witch in my own right, as a healer for the most part.

But it was my father's legacy that had set me on the path I was currently on, both figuratively and literally.

When I was sixteen years old, my dad had been killed by poachers, while he'd been trying to work towards conservation of magical habitats. Ever since then I had been determined that his legacy live on.

And that's why this particular group of poachers was interesting to me.

I had a hunch that they were the same ones that had killed my dad three years ago.

"I'm going to catch them this time, Dad," I promised. "They're never going to hurt another creature or person ever again."

It wasn't a vain vow. I knew enough about magic, having been around it my whole life, never to make a promise out loud that I wasn't going to be able to keep. I had vowed to bring my father's killers to justice.

It was the kind of vow that was totally unbreakable.

I would succeed or literally die in the attempt.

Under my arm, Fred kept up a commentary in a series of low clucks. I couldn't tell if he approved or disapproved of my hiking skills.

Who knows, maybe he was just singing some kind of camping song.

I was halfway up a particularly steep embankment when I came across the first sign that I might actually be on the right track. A tuft of pink hair was caught on a low-hanging branch, a shade of pink rarely seen in nature outside of newborn piglets. Only a truly Magical creature would ever be quite this pink.

I picked up my pace.

Maybe I'd get lucky this time, I thought to myself. Maybe I would be in time.

I almost was.

I would probably wonder for the rest of my life how things would have been different, had I come up the slope a few minutes earlier.

Instead, I walked into a massacre.

I gagged as I took in the vivisected corpses around me. Whoever had done this had not completed their work. All of the tusks of the mastodons had been removed and were gone, but only one of the bodies had been skinned and the pelt was still there, next to it.

What a sickening, useless waste.

Four miniature mastodons lay dead in the middle of nowhere, and I was the only one that seemed to care.

I knelt down beside one of the bodies, feeling tears stream down my cheeks. I hated crying. I hated feeling weak, but this time I couldn't help it. I scrubbed my face and focused on getting mad instead of sad.

The scene had been so similar, three years ago. The hacked up carcasses of the nearly extinct mastodons, the waste.... Only, last time my dad had been there, too, and they had killed him.

"So close," I muttered. "So very close."

I shied a rock at Fred, who was lapping at a pool of blood. "Leave it alone," I told him.

I dragged the corpse closest to me towards the one that had been skinned.

"They deserve better than this," I told Fred, who regarded me with one of his most jaded expression as if to ask me why I was allowed to play with the meat, and he wasn't. "I'm going to build a funeral pyre. I don't suppose you're much help." I huffed under the weight of the mastodon. This one had been full grown and probably would have stood at nearly three feet tall. It took every ounce of my strength—and a little earth magic—just to move him.

Fred settled down to watch me work.

"I should have named you 'Useless'," I told him as I started dragging the second body, a juvenile male, toward the pile I was forming.

Fred clacked his beak at me, offended.

The last body belonged to a mature female. I frowned as I regarded her still form. With so few miniature mastodons left in the world, this one female was worth so much more alive than dead.

Which was something the poachers would never understand. All they answered to was the siren call of the almighty dollar. It blinded them to the rare beauty of these majestic creatures.

Soon there wouldn't be any left in the world at all.

"Why are people such freakin' idiots?" I asked Fred, catching my breath before I tried to move this last pachyderm. "Why is everyone so blind? They're the ones that should be killed, not these innocent creatures."

Fred cocked his head at me.

"Don't even think about it," I warned him. "You set one fluffy feather out of line and the authorities will sweep in and it will be the blowtorch for you. You're not so bad, for undead poultry. Let's keep you undead a little longer, ok?"

Fred settled back down to watch.

I really hoped that meant he was agreeing with me.

I bent to grab onto the dead female and... something moved.

I bit back a shriek and swallowed hard.

I wasn't a wimp, but I really didn't like maggots, which were the only things I could think of that could make a clearly dead elephant move.

The movement came again, followed by a strange snuffling whimper sound.

"Oh," I breathed, stooping to push aside some of the female's heavy fur, "it's a calf!"

The little mastodon was tiny, and young enough that its lavender-tinted baby fur hadn't fallen out yet, which meant it had to be only days or weeks old. It was so tiny! I'd seen bigger Chihuahuas.

And it was a female.

"Oh," I repeated, absolutely stunned as a pair of sapphire-blue eyes stared up into mine.

She was just beautiful.

She let out a sad little trumpeting sound, running her impossibly tiny trunk through her dead mother's fur.

I swallowed the lump in my throat.

"I'll take care of you, Little One," I promised.

Suddenly all my goals shifted. I had to get this baby out of here before the poachers came back and found us here.

Nothing mattered anymore except getting the little one to safety. As much as I regretted abandoning the desecrated bodies of the calf's herd, they were no longer my priority.

I used my sword to hack off a chunk of the mother's fur to wrap the baby elephant in.

"Don't even think about hurting her," I snapped to Fred as he came towards us, curious about the funny noises coming from the tiny creature.

He puffed up his feathers, offended.

I quickly ripped open my pack and pulled out my map and spare clothes to make room for the baby mastodon. I stowed her in the pack with the tuft of her mother's fur inside of it. She wrapped her truck around the fur and made that horrible sad sound again.

"I'll have Iris make it into a blankie for you," I promised the baby. "Iris owes me, anyway."

Fred made a creeling sound at me.

"No, I haven't forgotten you," I told him. I tucked my clothes back around the baby and held out my arms to him. "Come on, we have to get out of here as fast as we can."

Fred hopped into my arms and settled himself down for the long trip.

I closed my eyes, calling the Earth magic around me, picturing the safety of my little apartment.

There was a sickening lurch, the world turned on its side beneath me.

And then we were home.

Chapter Two

I had no idea what to do. I had a baby elephant in my backpack. A critically endangered baby mastodon, at that.

I didn't know how to get access to what she needed to eat, or how to take care of her, but I knew I could get in a lot of trouble for having her in my apartment.

I bit my lower lip.

While in law school, I had spent a summer working for a judge down at the Magical courts. While there I had come across the mention of the most prestigious environmental lawyers that the Magical community had to offer, the Baehrs.

If anyone would know what to do for my little orphan, it would be them.

"Hold on," I told my little family. "We're going on another trip." I speared Fred with my most serious glare. "We're going to Magic Central. Behave yourself, OK? One false move and it's blowtorch time!"

Fred hissed at me.

"Nice," I told him, "I try to save your life and this is the thanks I get? Remind me to put onions on your next hamburger."

The room lurched again and I opened my eyes to the busiest place in the whole Magical world.

Magic Central was as big and busy as all of the major train stations in the world scrambled together...and then fed on steroids for a few years. Magical creatures and peoples of every variety moved at a fast pace, all headed in a different direction.

I started forward and almost bumped off of the stomach of a troll.

"Sorry," I murmured. "I wasn't looking where I was going."

"Quite all right," he answered, letting me pass.

I grinned to myself. Not all trolls were, well...trolls.

I dug into my pack for my map. I only had a vague idea of where the Baehr offices were. I ruffled around the baby elephant, who was snoring soundly, but there was no map anywhere.

"Crap," I whispered. "Where did I leave that thing?"

I'd just have to find my own way.

All the legal offices were lined along the same boulevard, near the main detention center. I headed that way and hoped that I'd recognize the office when I saw it.

I was in luck. They had a sign hanging outside of it with a bear on the sign.

I chuckled at the pun on their names, shaking my head, and pushed the door open.

The water-nymph secretary smiled openly at me as I entered. "Hello," she greeted. "I'm Willow. Welcome to

Baehr, Baehr, and Baehr Attorneys-At-Law. What can I we do
to help you?"

"I need to see a lawyer," I said. "I mean, I am a lawyer,
but I need to see an expert in Magical environmental law.
Well," I sighed, "can I please speak to one of the Baehrs?"

"Any preference?" she asked.

I shrugged. "Not really."

She pressed a button on her desk. "Kodi," she murmured,
"there's someone here to see you, a Miss..." She raised her
eyebrows at me.

"Locke," I told her, "Goldie Locke."

Her eyebrows rose further, but she relayed the
information.

I didn't have to wait long.

A tall and very irate man came down the hallway. "Look,"
he bellowed, the veins standing out on his forehead. "We're a
real, hard-working legal firm. We don't need jokesters
coming in here making fun..." He paused as he took in my
appearances.

"I mean no disrespect," I told him seriously. "My name is
really Goldie Locke. That I need your help is just...fortuitous."

He rubbed his jaw. "Your name really is Goldie Locke?"

I nodded. "Golden Sunshine Locke," I supplied helpfully.

His face cleared. "You're Daniel Locke's daughter, aren't
you?"

I nodded, relieved that he had recognized me.

"Come on in," he offered, gesturing down the hall. "I'm
sorry I overreacted."

"That's OK," I told him. "If my last name was Baehr and someone claimed to be Goldie Locke, I think I would have the same reaction."

He actually chuckled.

Now that he wasn't enraged, he had a cheerful expression and moved down the hallway with a carefree easy-going manner. He was taller than average, not that everyone didn't tower over my petite five feet nothing, with huge hands and a frame that should have been awkward, but somehow wasn't.

He ushered me into a small conference room and seated himself on the edge of the table, letting one of his long legs swing. "How can I help you, Ms. Locke?"

"Actually," I corrected him. "It's Dr. Locke, but that's not important at the moment."

He pursed his lips. "MD?"

I shook my head. "Two Ph.Ds and a law degree," I corrected.

He blinked at me. "But," he protested, "forgive me, but you look like you couldn't be older than seventeen."

Well, it was better than the usual assumed thirteen.

"I'm nineteen," I told him. "I started college when I was thirteen. It's a long story." I gave him a pointed look. "And that's not why I'm here."

I set my pack on the table and moved the mastodon fur aside to show the baby sleeping inside.

"Her herd is dead," I said.

"Oh, crap," Kodi Baehr said, taking in all the implications instantly.

I nodded. "Exactly."

I had to put it to the Baehrs. Once they had a handle on the situation they moved pretty darn fast. Kodi pulled up everything he could find on the care of endangered species and had me filling out forms that would allow me to legally foster the calf, while the older brothers somehow pulled strings that managed to get me supplied with everything I might need to take care of my new baby. That included alicorn milk, which was the closest Magical alternative to mastodon milk we had available.

"Are you sure you can take this on?" Kodi asked me, as I gathered my things together and prepared to go back home.

I shrugged. "What's the alternative?" I answered. "There are no zoos or preserves that could take her on. It's pretty much me or nothing."

He nodded ruefully. "Unfortunately you are correct."

"I can handle one little elephant," I told him confidently.

"Well, if you need any help, we're available," he told me with an open smile. He handed me a sheaf of papers. "Here's the contact information for the milk-donor, for when you run out. I've included all our contact information, and my personal cell." His smile broadened. "You can call me on it any time of night or day."

Oh, brother.

"Thanks," I said briskly. I tucked Fred back under my arm and headed back out to the streets of Magic Central.

"Good luck!" Kodi called after me.

"I can handle this," I repeated.

Chapter Three

"I don't think I can handle this," I told Fred as I paced around the house with a huge bottle and a whimpering baby elephant.

I was covered in milk and less-attractive fluids and the baby mastodon hadn't downed even half a bottle. Already she was looking weak and sickly.

"Drink," I coaxed her. "Please, little girl. You can't give up. A whole species depends on you to grow up and reproduce!"

Yeah, I needed to work on my pep-talks.

The little one clutched a tuft of fur in her trunk. She held it against her cheek like a toddler would their blankie.

She missed her mama.

I was a sorry substitute.

I slumped back into my rather lumpy easy chair and rocked her back and forth. What was that song Mom used to sing to the twins?

Hush, hush, time to be sleeping
Hush, hush, dreams come a-creeping
Dreams of peace and of freedom
So smile in your sleep, little baby

The little pink elephant seemed to like the sound of the song. I stuck the bottle into her mouth the second her jaw unclamped and squeezed a little of the warm milk onto her tongue.

She may have actually swallowed instead of spitting it out. There was no way I was going to stop singing now.

Eat, eat, eat little mastodon
Eat, eat, soon it will be dawn
Drink your bottle until its gone
I will protect you, sweet baby

The little elephant's huge brilliant blue eyes stared up at me.

"You're like a little flower," I decided. "I'm going to call you Petunia!"

"Aw," said a decidedly unfriendly voice behind me. "How cute and snuggly we are!"

I whirled around to see three sets of eyes staring down at me.

"I really hate being called cute," I said conversationally, wishing I had my sword within reach instead of across the room on the table. "You must be the poachers. How did you find me?"

The leader held up a familiar and well-folded piece of manuscript.

"Now it decides to be helpful?" I muttered.

Betrayed by my own map.

I caught Fred's eye from where he was perched on top of my bookshelf. Either the men hadn't seen him when they arrived, or they had assumed he was a stuffed bird.

"I could use a little help," I told him.

Freakin' rooster just disappeared.

"Onions," I muttered. "If I survive this I'm going to be showering that chicken with onions."

"Not to interrupt your soliloquy," the leader said, "but we'll take that little mastodon calf now."

"Not a chance," I snapped, tightening my hold on the little bundle in my arms. "I just barely got her eating. Do you think I'm just going to hand her over to you?"

The leader blinked. "Yes, actually I do." He shook his head. "What's a cute little thing like you going to do to stop us?"

I ground my teeth. "I really hate the term 'cute'," I told them. "It's belittling."

"Little," one of the guys, the one with the yellow teeth, snorted.

I narrowed my eyes at him and he looked at the ground.

"Take it," the leader said.

"Stupid move," I told him.

Clutching the baby bundle in one arm, I made a dive for my table and my sword. My fingers closed on the blade just as one of the men grabbed my ankle.

I kicked hard.

Yellow-Teeth yelped.

I whipped myself around, pointing my sword towards all three men. "Don't make me mad," I warned them.

"Aw," the leader said, "she's like a tiny little kitten. Maybe we should keep her...as a pet."

I glared at him.

I tapped into my powers. I could hear the earth magic thrumming below me, several stories down. It felt like it wanted to be called, as if the earth itself were angry with these poachers, these men who had violated her and killed her precious ones.

I just opened myself up as a conduit for its rage. Power roared through me, lashing around the three poachers.

It was echoed by another roar.

The last thing I remembered was the leader screaming as a giant bear appeared from nowhere and ripped his head off.

I awoke in my armchair and immediately sat up, looking for my little elephant.

"She's here," said a soothing voice. Big hands pushed the little bundle towards me.

A tiny pink trunk reached out of the blanket and wrapped itself around my ponytail.

I looked down at Petunia with a tender smile. Her beautiful blue eyes stared trustingly up into mine.

"Looks like you've been adopted," said the strange man kneeling beside me.

I frowned. "I'm sorry, but... Who are you?"

He smiled. "I'm Braun... Braun Baehr."

"Your zombie chicken came for us," added another voice. I looked up to see the familiar face of Kodi Baehr behind his brother. There was another man next to him, who I assumed was the third brother.

"Fred?" I asked, incredulously.

My zombie chicken sat sullenly in the middle of the kitchen table.

"He was actually...useful?" I demanded. "Isn't that against the zombie code, or the chicken code or something?"

Braun chuckled.

"I owe you," I told the rooster. "I'm going to take you to the butcher shop and get you anything you want...as long as it isn't chicken!"

"You never stop talking, do you?" Kodi said with a grin.

I grinned back. I was too relieved to be alive to even care that grinning made me appear even cuter than usual. "Nope," I admitted. "When you're my size, talking is the best offense."

"As in, 'the best defense is a good offense'?" Kodi teased.

My opinion of him rose considerably at that comment.

"So, what happened here?" I asked. "Since I apparently passed out."

"When we got here," Braun answered, "You had all three men bound up with earth magic so tightly they were being squeezed to death."

"Remind me never to made you mad," Kodi muttered.

"We had little choice, but to...put them out of their misery," the third man said.

"They were known criminals, Paul," Braun said over his shoulder to his brother. "I doubt the Council of Magic will take issue with us taking justice into our own hands."

"Paws," Kodi corrected cheerfully.

"Paws?" I closed my eyes against the memory of the huge bear. "You guys are...werebears?"

"She's sharp," Braun said in appreciation.

"Well," I said. "Thanks for coming to my rescue."

"Unnecessarily," said the man Braun had called Paul.

The little elephant in my arms started to wiggle. I grabbed her bottle from Braun and stuffed it into her mouth.

I grinned with relief as she started to suck milk down.

Now we were getting somewhere.

"I'm impressed," Braun said, "with how you handled yourself and your dedication to magical wildlife."

"This was personal," I said, trying not to look at a rather ugly stain near my kitchen table. I was pretty sure it was blood, though there were no other signs of the poachers. "They killed my father."

Braun nodded. "Daniel Locke," he said. "He used to work with us."

I blinked at him. "He did?"

Kodi nodded.

"Which is why we wanted to see if you would like to work with us in the same capacity," Paul announced seriously.

"What kind of position?" I asked suspiciously.

"Wildlife intermediary," Braun said calmly.

My eyes narrowed. "What does that even mean?"

"Oh," Kodi said calmly, swinging his leg, "it means rescuing Magical creatures and kicking poacher butts on a regular basis."

"That," I said willingly, "I can do."

Work of Art

I could not get this guy's attention.

Every day he came to the University art class where I was volunteering as a model, sat down, stared at me, drew my picture, and then disappeared. Every day I tried to give him some message with my eyes or with even a little twitch of my Magic that I wanted to talk to him.

But every day he just disappeared with his sketchbook, not even lingering to say hello to the person posing for him.

Dude, so rude.

I'd even gone so far as to leave him a note, but he just read it, looked around the classroom as if he were completely befuddled, and then stuffed the note into his pocket— apparently forgotten.

Even if he hadn't been drawing me for class, I was kind of hard to miss. I'm naturally blond, but currently my hair was multi-colored—as in, it was a rainbow. Since I was named after the goddess of rainbows, Iris, this was one of my favorite hairstyles.

Plus, I thought it suited me. Dang it, I'd been told that I was riveting, fascinating, gorgeous. I'd been called exotic and exciting.

But this guy? Apparently I didn't even register on his radar after he was done drawing me.

I wasn't sure what I saw in him anyway. Yes, he was attractive. He always wore these ratty jeans with real paint on them—not those phonied-up jeans that celebrities pay thousands to get pre-painted—and tousled hair. Heck, he even had that moody dramatic look to his face. As if at any moment he might sigh or throw his work across the room and scream at everyone.

OK, so I'm kind of into those dark and broody guys.

Look at me, I wanted to shout. Not just as lines for drawing, but me, the person sitting up here freezing off her buns in the name of art.

And time was running out. My tenure as model for the art class was drawing—pun intended—to a close. One more class period and I wasn't going to get to see him again.

I slathered paint all over my palette, ready for a distraction. These days I was focusing on still-life paintings of inanimate objects, not because I loved to paint them, or even because I was trying to work on my technique, but mostly because of my little Magical quirk, which made painting anything else a little...risky.

My art tended to come alive on the page.

Literally.

And, as even paint and paper animals tend to rampage, fruits and vegetables were a safer alternative to giving up art altogether.

And I had no intention of ever doing that.

It wasn't just with my art that things tended to go awry. Most things I did Magically ended up going bad. Sometimes I thought I'd been cursed. That mural that flooded my sister's house? Yeah, there'd been no intention there of bringing that waterfall to life. The damage that my 'art' had caused to her house? Yeah, that had been pretty permanent.

What was even worse was the backfire of my clean-up spell which had managed to raise the flood levels considerably.

Hence the painting of fruit baskets.

Nobody complained when painted fruit baskets came to life—even if the fruit did tend to turn to dust within a day. The worst complaint I ever got was that my bananas tasted like paper.

Which is kind of what you had to expect if you were going to eat someone's painting.

When I was little, I'd always loved my 'gift'. What child wouldn't love walking down the beach and drawing in the sand only to have the sketch come alive and play? Well, at least until the next stiff breeze came by. It had been exciting. My imagination literally came to life in front of my eyes every day.

It was when I was older that all the disasters started weighing on me.

It wasn't really my fault that that sketch in Herbology 101 had peeled off of the page and attacked my professor, right? Or that storm of flowers outside of my house that practically smothered all of us before they turned to dust? Even when I was cautious, things just got out of control.

And, as it tended to happen, my Magic was getting stronger as I got older. At twenty-three I was hardly at my Magical prime, which was generally at the age of ninety or a hundred and fifty or somewhere in the middle of that range.

I was painting to try to distract myself from the man of my dreams who was determined to ignore me, but it wasn't really helping. Instead, I kept seeing his face in my head. I was so distracted that I messed up mixing my colors, which I hadn't done in years. One thing I never messed up was getting that perfect shade of whatever color I needed.

It was almost Magical. Well, not 'almost'. I always felt safe using my Magic for that. It wasn't like finding the perfect shade could backfire on me.

At least, it hadn't yet.

I finished my painting just as class came into session. As the paint on the canvas began to dry, the painting peeled away, coming alive. I reached out and caught a pear just before it hit the floor.

I blew on it slightly, letting my Magic saturate every part of it. It was perfect. It felt like a pear in my hand, it smelled like a pear. I knew that if I ate it it would even taste like a pear.

What would I be able to do with a gift like that if I had it under control? If it weren't for the fact that everything I touched always turned to dust, sometimes literally, I could do great things. Maybe I could end world hunger? Maybe I could literally paint houses for the homeless.

The possibilities should have been endless.

I looked down at the pear in my hand. I'd painted with oils, so it should last at least a few hours before it started to turn to dust. Until then it would have a life, albeit a short one, as an actual pear.

I always wondered what happened to the art food I ate. Did it revert to paint and paper in my stomach, or did it have the nutrients of the fruit it appeared to be?

The creatures I drew seemed so real. They didn't obey me, but they flitted and flew and ran like the real things. As far as I could tell, they lived, even if it was only for a short time.

The better the art, the longer they lasted, and the more real they appeared to be. Sketches might only last a few seconds, depending on the medium I created them in—pen lasted longer than pencil—but detailed drawings could last for days, weeks.

I'd even kept one particularly well-drawn rabbit for a month before she'd faded and blown away on the wind.

Ursula, my bumble-bee bat, chirped from her perch on the outside of my ear. She and the rabbit had become close friends over that month. I knew she and I both missed that furry little busy body greeting us at the door every night when we got home.

Ursula spent most of her time sleeping on my ear, looking to most like a cuff, or hiding in my hair. Only at night was she alert.

I wondered what had caught her attention this time.

I turned. Ah.

It was him—my dream guy. I stifled a deep gut-wrenching sigh. Why couldn't I get him to look my way? Only when I was on the pedestal would I even exist for him.

I went behind the screen the professor had provided for me to change into my 'costume'. It was a filmy, drapy sort of thing—the kind that Greek goddesses supposedly wore to lounge around. There was no way anyone got anything else done.

Once I was dressed, I settled myself on the pedestal. It took forever, and a little bit of Magic, to get the folds to fall just right. I had to be as identical as possible to how I'd been the day before and the day before that.

Posing for artists was always an interesting experience. Some were very aware that I was a person. Those were the ones that fumbled and blushed as they worked. They avoided my eyes, or, on rare occasion, winked at me or tried to engage me into some sort of communication.

Then there were the artists that completely ignored the fact that I was a living, breathing person. They worked with simple fanaticism, their eyes never straying from their work. Their focus was scorching, intense. But me? I was an object, not a person.

Of course, those were the extremes. Most artists fell somewhere in between.

My dream guy, naturally, was one of those objectifying artists. He drew and painted, his gaze inwardly drawn. His eyes laid me bare, but coldly and meticulously, almost medically.

I was a piece of technical challenge, no more.

Since he was so oblivious to me, I felt free to stare at him as much as I wanted. How could anyone be so perfect? His mouth curled up on one side as he worked, his hair falling into his fanatic's eyes.

He was so deep, so broody.

So very very my type.

This time, I promised myself, I would do it. I would cross the room after class and ask him out. I would throw myself in front of his moving feet, if that were the only way I could get his attention.

Hopefully I wouldn't have to do anything that drastic. These drapes weren't made for that kind of drama.

I spent the rest of the session daydreaming about our lives together—from our first date to our third child and lovely Alaskan-frontier getaway. I was so immersed in my own head that I nearly missed class ending, and my opportunity to accost, er, seduce my wayward prince charming.

I hopped off of my pedestal and ran after him, nearly tripping over my skirts in the process.

That's all I needed, to literally fall head-over-heels for him.

"Wait," I called, gathering my skirts together.

He turned toward me just as he entered the doorway. Our eyes met for an instant.

A shock of recognition shot through me.

It was enough time to allow him to walk through the door and disappear.

I ran after him into the hallway, but it was too late.

He was gone.

I put my hand over my heart, feeling the way it was thundering in my chest. Could it really be true? How could something like this have happened?

I knew that face so well. Surely I was imagining it.

I turned back to the classroom and grabbed up my sketch pad.

Page after page I turned, looking down at some sketches half-finished, just waiting for a few more lines before they would come to life.

Half-way through the pages I found it.

I found him.

My dream guy.

I sat down on the floor, staring down at the lines I had created. How could I have forgotten? How could I not have seen?

He was perfect for me.

Because I had created him.

Starrie Crossed

I am not my own worst enemy, but I am pretty close to it. In my opinion, everyone probably is the same way. And my opinion is usually right, anyway. I know that sounds like I'm bragging, but it's actually the truth.

My mom said I was born looking to get into any trouble I could. I'm not sure if she thinks I was born bad, or if she just despairs because I always do things my way. Sometimes my way doesn't make other people happy.

Sometimes I play pranks. A girl has to keep herself busy, after all.

It's just so easy to get what I want, when I know exactly what makes a person tick.

So, maybe that makes me a con artist. That was only one of my father's many tricks. Maybe it was hereditary along with his silver eyes, which my twin sister, Rainy, and I both have.

Rainy and I are beyond the usual identical as far as twins go. Sometimes I think we breathe in synchronized chorus. We can pretty much hear what the other is thinking, too. Even our fingerprints and, I'm assuming, our retinas, are identical.

Only Magical twins create clones like that. Heck, even clones get something of their own.

Sometimes, like when I'm asleep, I almost forget which one of us I am. It's super creepy. So, when I wake up, I try to be as much myself as I can.

I don't want me to disappear.

That makes it sound like I resent my twin, which is far from the truth. We understand each other perfectly. I love her... well, as much as I love myself. Because we're the same 'self' anyway.

We do try to give each other some privacy and space, but when we sleep our brains do that Magic twin stuff again and we wake up sharing all kinds of memories.

Even some stuff that I'd rather not share.

I've gotten pretty good at blocking those into the 'pretend that never happened' part of my brain.

Denial's good for people. I'm a big believer in it.

Because I'm so big on being me and not vanishing, I guess I have a tendency to walk into situations that I should have been able to avoid. No, maybe I didn't need to pass out a Magical wedgy to that jogger who passed us—good luck getting that one out—but, then again, he didn't have to whistle at me, either.

So, I've got that side of me—the fearless, brash, thrill-seeker.

But I've got another side.

Deep, deep, down.

Because I think down at that level that my mother might be right about me.

What if I really was born... evil?

Sometimes I feel like there's this lump inside of me, like a glowing black pearl of power. I can feel its energy and I know that I could tap into it and be even stronger than I am.

And my sister and I are pretty awesome witches. We've got spells and ideas figured out that have stumped others for centuries.

No, seriously not bragging here. We're pretty brilliant.

But I think this pearl, this darkness inside of me, would make me even stronger.

Everyone jokes about which one of us is the evil twin.

I think it might be me.

That temptation of power is always there. I can feel it sitting heavily deep inside me. Sometimes I think I can hear it calling to me.

Sometimes I think that I'm just a little nuts to think that any such thing exists.

This was the one thing that I kept from Rainy. If she'd picked up on any of my anxiety over it, she never said anything.

I didn't let myself wonder who I would be, if I ever succumbed to the temptation of all that power.

I wasn't thinking about it at the moment. Rainey and I were on a 'date', which meant that we were out on the town together getting dinner and a movie and acting like single women do. After the movie we had big plans to hit up my sister's bakery for some chocolate and sugar before heading home just in time not to incur our mother's wrath.

Mom did wrath like nobody else.

We were about halfway through the parking lot, talking about the special effects of the movie we'd seen, when a car came screeching around the corner. As it shrieked away, past us, I saw something large and dark thrown clear.

"Oh, my gosh," Rainey shrieked. "I think it's a body!"

I suppose at that moment we could have either turned away and pretend we hadn't seen anything, or we could run to help.

We never took the easy way out. We ran to where the—yes, it looked like a body—was lying in the middle of the parking lot.

My first thought was that it was dead. I really didn't want to touch someone who was dead. It wasn't that I hadn't seen dead people before or anything. I just didn't like touching anything that was dead. Heck, I didn't even like touching wooden furniture because it was made from dead trees.

What, so I have issues.

Just as we were close enough that one of us was going to need to do something, the body began to moan and thrash around.

Rainey froze on the spot, so I pushed past her, grabbed the nearest shoulder and rolled the person over.

It was a guy, that much I could tell, even in the darkness. The rest was pretty much hidden by all the blood. Had he gotten that beaten up by his fall from the car, or had he been injured before he was thrown clear? I couldn't tell.

But I did know enough to know he needed our help right away.

"Rainey," I said. "Call 911. Tell them what happened."

My sister nodded, fishing out her cellphone.

Electronics tended to burn out quickly with witches like us, but we had service through a Magically aware company, so this was yet another replacement for a Magical blow-up. I heard her talking in a low voice as I leaned over the injured guy.

I needed light.

"Damn it, Starrie," I said to myself. "Are you a witch or not? Stupid, stupid girl." It took barely a thought before the whole area was lit up by a fairylight.

I winced as I looked down. The guy wasn't going to be able to wait for the paramedics. There was so much blood everywhere that I could tell he didn't have much time.

"You're lucky we were here," I told him, not caring if he could hear me or not.

I placed my hands over his chest and drew my Magic through me.

I wasn't really a healer, not like my sister, Goldie, but I knew enough to let the Magic do what it would. If I tried to direct the healing, I would probably do more harm than good.

Instead, I was just a conduit of positive energy into him.

As I focused all my power on him I felt the strangest thing. It felt as if that pearl—that darkness—inside of me was lightening. The pearl wasn't exactly leaving me, but it didn't feel so heavy or so foreboding.

Something about this guy was making the evil deep inside of me start to fade.

I looked down at him, looking at his face for the first time, trying to understand what it was.

He was a young guy, probably our age or a little older. His face was drawn and pale from all the blood he had lost, but he was still not-bad looking. I probably would have given him a second glance if we hadn't met in such unfortunate circumstances.

And, while I was watching his face, the jerk decided to stop breathing on me.

"Oh, no you don't," I growled, pulling more and more Magic from the Earth around us to feed into his system. "You are not going to die. I absolutely forbid it."

I felt it immediately when Rainey's Magic joined my own. Together we poured a flood of more and more power into a guy who was determined to die.

Well, I wasn't going to let that happen.

I pressed my mouth against his and blew deeply into his lungs, not just air, but pure, raw power. If he had been conscious it would have hurt worse than a thousand sunburns.

Two more times I drew in my breath and Magic and poured them into him.

The last time I felt his lips move beneath mine just as he drew in a gasping, agonizing breath.

As he stared up at me, I felt like my power was a beacon of moonlight glowing beneath my breastbone.

I opened my mouth to ask him why he had that effect on me, but that was when the paramedics arrived. They brushed us efficiently aside, scarcely listening to a word we said, and set to whisking our stranger away.

In a matter of moments we were left alone, in the middle of the parking lot, wondering what kind of freight train had just run us over.

"Well," I said shakily. "A girl always dreams of her first kiss. I don't know. I guess I thought the guy would be alive when I kissed him."

Rainey looped her arms around my shoulders, hearing the words that I wasn't saying. We drew in a deep breath together.

Together felt nice.

I was drained and exhausted.

I wanted to go home.

Without a word, Rainey and I linked our little fingers and invoked the Magic that would take us home.

Our car could wait for later.

Right now we needed to recoup.

And wonder what it was about the guy that had made my Magic shine. Already it was darkening again. I could feel it dim, curling in on itself inside of the deepest recesses of my heart.

Whatever he had done, it wasn't permanent.

It was three days later that I saw the headline over my stepfather's shoulder as he read the news on an actual newspaper at the table.

"Wait," I said, before he could turn the page.

Rainey and I hovered over the paper as we quickly scanned the contents of the article.

We stared at each other.

"We saved the life of a fugitive?" Rainey's voice was high with stress.

"A hacker suspected in a murder case," I said numbly.

"Yes," Stephan, our stepfather, said, oblivious to our connection to the man in the article. "He's allegedly connected to at least three murders of young women in the area."

I sat down in the nearest chair.

I'd aided someone who didn't deserve it—someone who was evil.

What if that's why my Magic had responded to him like that? What if it hadn't been brightening up because he was healing me, but brightening because it sensed its own in him.

I felt sick. I wanted to scrub my mouth out. I had breathed life into him.

"We didn't know," Rainey said softly.

"I know," I answered. "It doesn't make me feel any better. What if we saved him just to let him hurt more people?"

"We're not responsible for his action," Rainey said firmly, her chin resting on the top of my head.

I drew in a shuddering breath. "You weren't the one who breathed life into him, Rainey. It was me."

"So we should have let him die?"

"No!" I shouted the word so loudly her eyes widened into silver saucers of astonishment. "No, we couldn't let him die. I don't know, It's just..."

I had thought I'd found my salvation in saving him.

Instead, I thought I'd just found my fate.

The dark pearl inside my chest pulsed, teasing me with the power it contained. It taunted me, knowing more than I did who I really was.

No matter how hard I tried it would always be there, waiting for a weak moment.

If I ever let my guard down, it would be there to awaken the dark inside of me.

Roses Red

My garden was my favorite place in the entire world.

My mother had named me accurately when I was a baby. All I loved, all I felt connected to, were these plants surrounding me. They fed my soul and I poured my Magic into them. It was a dance much like the dance of Nature herself.

I loved to surround myself with roses.

So, when I met a man who loved roses even more that I did, I knew he was the man I was going to marry.

The problem was, he was the one man I couldn't have.

Of course I fell in love with my Magical Herbology professor. As I thought about it, it was nothing but logical. Here I was, a doctorate candidate in my chosen field, surging forward with my life with no obstacles.

And the next thing I knew, the professor in my favorite spouted out this whole incredible story about why roses were so receptive to Magic and I fell in love.

Just like that.

And Dr. Redding was not the kind that broke rules. I doubted he even bent them on occasion. As long as I was his student he wouldn't even see me as a person.

And I wasn't that kind of person, either.

My path was clear.

I had to get my degree as quickly and efficiently as possible so I could ask Dr. Redding out on a date.

I was sure, when he saw my garden, that he would fall in love with me too.

Three years. Three years I slaved away, working hard, counting down to the moment that we would both be free. I just believed that we were meant for each other. He would still be un-entangled when I was finished, I just knew it. There was no way the fates would show me true love just to cast it away on the wind.

I just believed with my whole heart that we would be together.

Someday.

If life after doctorates actually existed.

In those long hours while I slaved away on my dissertation I would remind myself that he was waiting for me on the other side of this insurmountable task. I wrote about roses and Magic.

I wondered, when he read it, if he knew that I was writing it for us.

And then the day for my dissertation defense came. I went with shaking knees in front of the committee.

And he ripped me to shreds.

There, in front of my professors and peers. In front of all those I admired in my chosen field, he questioned and tore apart every section of my dissertation until I wanted to scream that it was all trash—all of it—even though it had taken me the better part of a year to write it to my standards.

But I didn't scream it. Instead, I quietly defended my work. I fought for that baby of paper and words. I answered every question I could, and admitted defeat when I was asked questions I had no answers to.

When it was all over, I had my degree.

But my heart felt like it had been shredded into a million pieces.

Had I been a fool all this time? Had I just been a silly school girl with a head full of fantasy and dreams?

I retreated to my garden. It should have been in victory, but instead I found myself in tears, shaking with all the exhaustion of those three long years.

I had been so sure.

I felt him enter my garden. This was my territory—I knew who he was the moment his foot entered my land.

"Have you come to take my degree away," I said bitterly.

He cleared his throat.

My mother had raised me to be polite. All that training forced me to turn and acknowledge him, though I was afraid my heartbreak was written all over my face.

"I had to do that," Dr. Redding said. "We both needed to know that you earned that degree—that I didn't just hand it to you. You needed to fight for it with tooth and claw."

I blinked at him through my tears. "I don't understand."

And then he kissed me.

My heart soared. I swore my roses started to sing.

I had been right! My true love was mine at last!

Fairytale Beginning

The last thing I ever expected was a fairytale ending to my love story. I mean, there was no such thing as Magic, to begin with, and then there's the whole issue with the fact that I am nothing like a fairytale princess, despite my love of pink. I'm a modern girl, despite my love of everything retro.

The carriage we were riding in was drawn by unicorns. I mean, real unicorns! They were huge, with thick crests and marble-colored muscles and tons of hair with shimmering horns that looked like metal sticking out of their heads.

I shook my head to myself. I couldn't wrap my brain around any of this stuff.

"What do you think?" My husband, Justice, wrapped his hand around mine and held it as if he were touching a treasure.

My husband. What an insane turn of events!

Prince Justice Courage Phillippe Jacobo Thyme the Third of the Middle lands, as he had introduced himself what felt like an age ago, was my real, live, Prince Charming.

And all of this Magic and beauty around me—that was all for a girl who didn't believe in True Love.

Or, at least, I hadn't until Justice had waltzed into my life and announced his betrothal to my best friend.

"Is any of this actually real?" I murmured to Justice, realizing he was waiting for an answer. "It's all far too good to be true."

He chuckled. When he smiled like that his face lit up like a small sun. There was no other word for it—Justice was pretty, even prettier than me.

I smoothed the skirt of my pink baby-doll dress and tried to calm the butterflies in my stomach. I was so ill-suited for this change of events. I wasn't a princess or even Magical.

I was, as my best friend, Cindy Eller would have put it, Ordinary.

What made me think that I could be a fairytale princess?

Justice grinned at me, squeezing my hand.

Oh, yeah. Him.

Justice loved me, for whatever reason. It was a good thing, because I loved him, too—completely and irrevocably.

"I have so much I want to show you," Justice said, gesturing out the window at the majestic view all around us. "All of this will be yours someday, when you are Queen."

I swallowed hard. Queen? I didn't even want to think about being Queen.

I could barely even handle being a wife.

The idea made me shiver, half from fear, half from delight. It had all happened so fast.

But here we were. It was real.

Our happily ever after.

I knew I was going to have to face the other stuff—the Queen stuff—at some point. But we were on our honeymoon. There was no way I was going to stress about that now.

And, though I couldn't wait to get Justice alone, I also felt nervous about that. He had risked so much for me. We had known each other for so short a time.

What if he regretted marrying me?

After all, I wasn't Magical. I was Ordinary in every sense of the word.

Yes, I was pretty. Everyone had always told me I was pretty from the time I was very small. But I knew that that sort of thing didn't guarantee love. And I knew that it wouldn't last. Nothing ever did 'stay gold'.

"Tansy," Justice said, in that tone of voice that always sent shivers down my spine. "Don't worry. You belong here."

That was just it. I knew I belonged here, more than I had ever belonged anywhere. If I couldn't make a life here, then I would never ever be able to find happiness.

That scared me. I'd wanted a home for so long.

It wasn't right to think of sad things on the happiest day of my life, but my thoughts turned to my parents.

My parents should have been there.

That was the story of my life.

The day I graduated from high school, my parents separated.

It had been a long time coming. I don't think anyone was surprised.

I walked out before they could kick me out, never to return. I knew if I didn't leave on my own, they would have to ask me to go, and I just didn't want to deal with that.

All I took with me were a few clothes, my favorite books— Pride and Prejudice, Great Expectations, my pink Bible, and the full works of LM Montgomery—and all the money from my bank account.

I didn't really have a place to go. All my friends were still living at home, planning for college and their promising futures.

I was glad to leave. I was sick of being ignored. I was sick of being a problem. I was sick of them always fighting about me.

The worst part was knowing that they wouldn't miss me. They would hardly even notice I was gone.

They didn't need each other. And they didn't need me.

Any love they must have felt for me had quickly turned to resentment. I had ruined their lives. I was never good enough. I had been an accident, unwanted.

Well, now they could pretend that I was an accident that never had happened. My parents were young enough. They could make a new start.

Without me.

Of course I felt sad. I was walking away from the only life I'd ever known. My parents had never overtly abused me. They just hadn't noticed me.

But I knew they wouldn't look for me, now that I was gone.

I did what any eighteen year old on her own did—I worked. I worked any and all jobs I could. I kept my head above water.

I did what I'd always done.

I survived.

It wasn't until I walked into a funny little bakery, looking for a job, that I found family in the form of two girls—Jessi and Cindy.

I couldn't have asked for better friends. With them I had what I'd always craved—that casual intimacy I'd always been denied. We lived together and snarked at each other in the mornings before I had my coffee. We stayed up late and ate buckets of ice cream and gossiped and cried together and laughed until we cried.

And I felt a piece of that broken part of me begin to heal. I started to think that maybe I was worth loving, after all.

It was thanks to Jessi and Cindy that I built enough confidence to face the world and challenge it instead of hiding myself away.

And it was thanks to Cindy that I had met Justice—because of her and Jessi that I hadn't run away at the thought of having a family, a marriage of my own.

Because, to me, marriage was what my parents had had—cold, devoid of any form of affection.

When Justice walked into my life I hadn't seen or heard from my parents in eight years.

I was damaged goods. How could someone like me, unlovable, ever have a happily ever after?

Maybe I couldn't, but at least I could try.

This wasn't my fairytale ending.

It was a beginning.

The castle loomed up in front of us. I knew it was there, but my eyes were on the prize—on Justice's face. No matter what struggled would come our way, I knew we would conquer them all together.

"Welcome home, darling," Justice said, his lips brushing against my forehead.

My hand tightened in his.

I was really, finally home.

From Guest Writers

The following stories are guest pieces from fan writers Rebekah Leeson and Peg Lewis. I hope you enjoy them as much as I did.

If you enjoy their work, please let me know on my Facebook page.

Puppy Love by Rebekah Leeson

That was it. I had officially had enough and if I heard one more whistle, catcall, or 'hey girl!' I was going to burst, and not in a pleasant way.

To every passing guy, I looked like any other normal teenage girl walking down the street. What they didn't know, and what we did our very best to keep Ordinaries from knowing, was that I was actually much, much more. With a simple swipe of my hand an obtrusive boy could very possibly end up having an extremely different lifestyle.

As I continued walking down the street a song from my favorite Broadway musical, Into the Woods, entered my mind. "I could have turned him into a stone, or a dog, or a chair." I giggled at how incredibly possible it would have been for me to do something like that. Oh, Bernadette, how could you understand me so perfectly?

Another mile and I had finally reached my destination. Fortunately, no one else had decided to comment on how attractive they thought I was. I pulled open the glass door and smiled at the woman behind the counter. "Hello Sherry," I said brightly, "how are things going?" She shrugged.

Sherry and I had begun working at Big Hearts, Little Hands Daycare at about the same time last year and our friendship had kind of sparked when we saw how similar we were. As the year moved on we had continued to find common grounds between us.

Sherry was four years my senior and was a young bride with a strapping husband and a baby on the way. She was one of those people who were almost always smiling, and I'm sure the baby helped. I mean, if you wanted to see in person the pregnancy glow that magazines always talked about, Sherry was the one to go to.

I swigged a quick drink from the water fountain and strode into the children's area. Big Hearts is a daycare of sorts taking care of children six months of age to 12 years. I mostly worked with the two-year olds. There was something about toddlers that just really pulled me in. They could express themselves in an understandable way without being snotty about it. I know that everyone feels differently about kids, but in my opinion they were by far the best age group to work with.

Kassie spotted me first. I watched as her face lit up. "Emma," she screamed. It didn't take long before everyone was racing toward me, excited to tell me everything that had happened to them since I'd seen them last, which was yesterday evening. There's nothing more satisfying than a horde of ecstatic children vying for a spot at your feet.

Kassie squeezed my knees and began screaming something about a picture she had painted. Her tiny voice was barely audible over the demands of the other boys and girls trying to be heard. I laughed and did my best to get them all to back up. "Alright, alright! One at a time, please. I can't understand all of you."

It took a little while, but eventually the children were seated and ready to take turns. Every witch's power focused in a different area, and mine was all about children. Kids understood magic in a different way than adults. They were more accepting of the possibility that perhaps the impossible really wasn't that improbable. Magic worked in a different way around them.

Cord raised his hand and I pointed at him. With a toothy grin spreading from ear to ear, he began to speak. "Miss Emma, guess what! I did it, I did it! You told me to do it and I did and guess what!" Every word gushed out before I had the chance to understand him. I motioned for him to slow down, and then told him to start over.

"I told you that I asked mommy for a puppy and she said no. You told me to ask my daddy, so I did, and guess what! I'm getting one!" I blinked. When I had told him yesterday that parents answers always differ from one another's I hadn't actually meant for him to ask his dad. I forgot all too often that children actually take you seriously and listen to every word you say. I hoped no trouble would be caused in the family because of me.

We went around and each child told me about their lives or showed me pictures they had colored or mumbled something unintelligible and I laughed along with them. Twenty minutes later, it was time for snack. Goldfish and juice sounded pretty good to my unfed belly.

Around four o'clock, Kassie suddenly shot up and pointed excitedly at the door. "Sam! Sam!" I turned to see who this Sam was and almost swooned as I caught sight of him. Talk about a hunk. Suddenly every boy I ever thought was attractive went out of my head.

Sam smiled as he walked in the door. "Hey Kass, how you doin'?" Kassie giggled as he scooped her up into the air. She wrapped her arms around his neck and he kissed her cheek before setting her down. She reached up for his hand and the two turned to go.

Every instinct in my body was screaming at me. "Run to him, he could be the one. Quickly now, you're running out of time!" Somehow, my mind was still intact enough to know that wasn't a good idea. Instead, I rapidly searched the room looking for any kind of excuse to get close to Sam.

"Kassie," I screamed before I had found something. Sam turned, his sandy hair swooshing ever so slightly from the sudden movement. I racked my brain trying desperately to ignore the constant shouting of my instincts. My hand sought the table beside me and I picked up a random paper. Looking at it, I realized that fortunately it was Kassie's. "Kassie," I said again, in a more conventional tone. I was fairly certain I was not controlling my legs and yet I was steadily moving toward her. "I think you forgot this," I said.

"Oh. Yep! Thanks Miss Emma." I smiled at her. As I stood up straight I felt Sam's eyes wandering over my body. I looked at him and almost melted. His smile was unbelievable. He was unbelievable. His eyes were deep blue and there was a warmth in them that I had never seen in anyone else.

He reached out his hand and my arm moved voluntarily. "Hey," he said. His voice was deep and smooth. "Name's Sam. I'm Kassie's older brother. We don't get to see each other very often so it's always exciting when we get the chance, huh li'l sis?" Kassie nodded. Could he be any more perfect?

"Yeah, but I'm in town for the summer so we'll be seeing a lot more of each other." Kassie squealed in delight. I did too. Unintentionally of course. How could I help it? I had the whole summer to try to get this guy to think that there was no other girl in Tucson... no in the whole state of Arizona, in all of the USA that was as perfect for him as I was. "Well," his voice brought me back from my reverie. "I guess that's goodbye."

"Oh yeah," I stammered. "I guess so. Will you be picking her up from now on then?" The words came out before I could stop them. "You know, since you're spending more time with her and everything," I added quickly, so as not to sound totally desperate. Haha! Too late for that. He chuckled. He was probably used to girls acting like they were complete idiots around him.

"Um, I don't know. My mom has this list of things she wants me to do while I'm around so I'll be pretty busy, but I guess we'll see." Something inside of me cracked at hearing that I may not be seeing him. What is wrong with me, I thought. Why am I acting like a fool? My self-inflicted reprimand was clearly doing nothing as I heard the next words come out of my mouth.

"Well, it'll be nice to see more of you." This time he full out laughed, while I died inside. Why couldn't my magic make me seem smart, or give me ability to win over any guy I wanted? Instead, I continued to make myself look absolutely wasted.

"It'll be nice to see you, too," he said. I smiled at him and then forced myself to turn away before I could make a bigger fool of myself. I heard the door open and shut behind me and then my I felt my body relax. I took a deep breath and determined to forget about this day, this moment, and this truly perfect boy named Sam.

A few weeks later, I was sitting shotgun waiting for my mom to exit Fry's Food and Drug. Katy was blaring on the radio and I was singing along with her at the top of my lungs in a voice that would make her...shrink and die in the back seat, but I didn't care. This was my song.

"So you wanna play with magic, boy you should know what you're falling for. Baby do you do dare to do this, 'cause I'm comin' at ya like a dark horse." I continued to sing through the chorus and then the second verse and then the chorus again. I was really getting into it.

The rap started and I suddenly became all too aware of another voice mixing with Juicy J's. I took a look out the window and gasped. Why? Was it really not possible for me to make a good impression with this guy?

Katy started singing again and Sam looked at me expectantly. I only stared back at him. He shrugged and his voice filled the car as he took up my part. "Are you ready for, ready for the perfect start, perfect start? 'Cause once your mine, once your mine, there's no going back."

The song ended and my hand shot to the power button. "Hey, why'd you turn it off? I wanted to hear the next song!" I was slightly taken aback by the complaint and thought about turning it back on, but I saw my mom walk out of the door and changed my mind.

Sam and I stayed in positions, the silence between us becoming more and more awkward as the seconds passed by. An eternity later, my mom showed up at the trunk and Sam jumped to help her. I opened my door and climbed out and began stuffing groceries into the car.

"Well thank you, young man but I'm afraid I haven't met you before. Emma, are you going to introduce me to your friend here," my mom asked.

"Oh, we're not friends," I said too quickly. Sam looked wounded. I scrunched my face in embarrassment. "Sorry. I meant that we weren't friends yet. I mean, I just met him." Sam suddenly stuck out his hand and my mom accepted it.

"What she means to say is I'm Sam. My parents divorced last year and my mom moved down here with my little sister Kassie who goes to the daycare your daughter works at." My mom smiled and handed him another bag.

"Well Sam, it's nice to meet you. We don't get many gentlemen around these parts. I'm glad you're here." I had never truly known what gratitude was until the moment that conversation ended. Once the groceries were all packed, I said goodbye and climbed back in. My mom's door opened and the car started up.

"Hey Emma." Sam was still there. I didn't think I could make a bigger fool of myself and so I risked a response. "Hey, I know we just met and all, but..." He was stumbling. Even so, he managed to still be totally adorable about it. "Well, okay, so..." I took a breath. "My mom asked me to go with her to this Ice Cream social thing her boss is putting on and I guess I'm supposed to bring a plus one and there's this girl that I really want to ask."

My heart stopped. I was no longer able to breathe and I was positive I was drowning. How dare he come in here as if he was going to ask me and then go on about some other girl? He was still over there naming off her traits and I wasn't listening. At least that's what I told myself. Unfortunately, it was hard to ignore someone like Sam.

"...she's really pretty and her hair is long and dark. It's actually just like yours." I suddenly became aware of his hand stroking my dark locks. Totally and completely unbelievable. I turned toward my mom and the car pulled forward. "Emma wait!" I rolled up my window resisting the urge to scream at him.

Our minivan was well out of the parking space when the car stopped unexpectedly. "What are you doing," I yelled at my mom. "Keep going!" My mom held up her hands and I could see that this was not of her doing. She turned the car off and then switched the key. The car started up and she put it in drive. She pushed on the gas and the car zipped...backwards. The kind of energy flowing through the tight space suggested that this was no ordinary problem. We had a witch on our hands.

I jumped out of the car with a spell in my head and my hands ready. Sam threw his hands into the air innocently and the car stopped. Suddenly, the car radio turned on and Katy was blaring again. Why was it that every popular radio station played the same six songs?

"So you wanna play with magic," I said along with her. "Alright. I always wanted a puppy." Magic coursed through me and blasted out of my fingers. Sam deflected it nicely, which meant that I would have a nasty headache and wouldn't even get a dog out of the deal. In a flash he was pressed against me.

"You were the one I was asking out, Emma. Gosh, don't be such a witch." Oh, haha, I thought. I bet that's how he gets all the girls. But luckily for me, he was much too close than was good for him. My magic always worked better when in direct contact with my victim. I touched his face and within seconds a puppy sat expectantly at my feet. I laughed as I looked at him. Sam actually made a very nice Shih Tzu.

Arizona isn't even on the top ten worst drivers list, but as the seventeen-year-old unlicensed girl I was I felt like it should have been. I had been in too many near life or death experiences than I cared for. Crossing the street felt like braving a battleground, my ever wary eyes looking around for the next car to dodge. Fortunately, none came.

A movement tiny movement caught my eye and I turned to catch a better glimpse. Two boys sat in the car directly beside me, both waving in a creepy come-over-here-and-try-me-out way. I ignored them and continued my stride to the other side. And then I heard the catcall. I waited until I was directly in front of their vehicle before facing them. My hand shot up and a spell came into my head. A honk from somewhere broke off my concentration and I looked around. Sam was in the car a few feet over. I quickly flipped my hand the other way modeling my very cute middle finger to the boys and ran over to Sam's car.

"Hey Em, I assume we're going to the same place. Kassie's in the back. Need a ride?" I gratefully hopped in, realizing too late that it did nothing for me for the other boys to see me get into another guy's car. Sam smiled at me and I giggled at the memory of leaving him a poor, abandoned Shih Tzu puppy. The light turned green and we were on our way.

"So, are you ready for tonight," he asked. You would have thought that after the whole parking lot incident he would have left me alone, but that wasn't the case. The next day, he called me up and asked me, in a normal way, if I would go with him to his mom's Social. I had, of course, accepted graciously. I had also learned that his mom was a witch, but his dad was an Ordinary and he was the only one of his siblings (two brothers ages 14 and 8, and Kassie) who had showed any promise in developing their power.

"Um yeah, I guess so," I said. "Um, thanks. For saving me back there I mean. I've had enough of the whole hey-hot-stuff-come-over-here thing. I don't know what I was thinking I would do to them but it very likely could have started the Tucson Witch Trials. And I'm pretty sure no one is prepared for that." He chuckled and I did too.

After my shift was over, I quickly changed in the bathroom and then waited, with Kassie, in the lobby. The social started at seven o'clock which was the same time I got off work, and so our plan was that Sam would wait 'til seven to pick up Kassie where he would pick up both of us and drop Kassie off at my house which was about a mile away from where the social was. My mom would take care of it from there.

I would like to say that the Social was fabulous and that I loved every second of it but that would be a lie and I was taught to never bear false witness. Everyone there except for Sam and I was over thirty and most were married and those who weren't were obviously single. The only good part of the night was, regrettably, the Ice Cream which was delicious. But of course it was. My cousin was, after all, the one who came up with the fabulous flavors Sweet Dreams Ice Cream made.

The drive back home was done in near silence. I was fine with that, and Sam seemed to be just fine too. At some point one of us turned on the radio and what do you know? Katy was just starting to sing. I began to sing along with her and then Sam played Juicy J and then it was back to me. By the end of the song there was more laughing than singing, but it felt good to finally laugh.

Tears came to my eyes as I realized that this was the happiest I had felt in a long time. My dad had worked for the Council of Magic and had gone on a business trip two years ago. Misfortune had stuck his nose in the way and no one had heard from my dad or those who were with him since. Some nights, my mom and I sat on the couch watching old movies eating Sweet Dreams Ice Cream comforting each other by saying that he'd be back at any moment. But deep down inside, we knew that each of us had accepted that he was probably dead, and we would never hear from him again.

The car stopped and I realized that I was home. Sam turned off the car and smiled at me. "Don't get out yet." He opened his door and slid across the top of the car like he was Michael Westen in Burn Notice and opened my door. I flashed a fake fan across my face and held my hand out in true princess fashion. Sam held my fingers and kissed them tenderly. "Mi'lady."

I rolled my eyes and stepped out of the car. He offered his arm and I took it. He gently led me up the steps and I opened my door. "Come on in," I offered. "Hopefully Kassie's asleep by now and will need a big, strong man like you to carry her out." Now it was his turn to roll his eyes. We walked in and as I had assumed, Kassie was asleep on the couch.

My mom came rushing down the stairs just as Sam was scooping Kassie into his arms. "Oh, Emma you look lovely!" she exclaimed as quietly as she could. I realized then that I hadn't actually seen my mom since that morning. When we had dropped off Kassie, Sam had brought her to the door and I had stayed in the car. My deep green dress was low cut with thin sleeves and stopped abruptly at my knees. My dark brown hair flowed over my shoulders, the gentle waves ending directly below my breast. I had gone for a natural look with my make-up using a shade of purple eye shadow that complemented my green eyes beautifully. I had to agree with her, I looked damn good.

Sam smiled at me. "I definitely agree with you there Mrs. Walters. Emma was by far the most radiant witch there." My mom beamed at the compliment. She didn't have to know that I was only woman there under thirty years of age.

Sam said goodnight and started out the door. "Hey Sam," my mom called out. "You should come for dinner sometime. It's always nice to get to know another witching family. What about next Friday?" Sam nodded and said that it was a great idea and he'd talk to his mom about it. I watched him buckle Kassie up, and then he hopped into the driver's seat and pulled away.

Thursday came along and I was panicking. Sam, Kassie, and their mom were all coming tomorrow since Sam's brothers lived in Salt Lake with his dad. I was more nervous than I could ever remember being. I had no idea what we were going to eat, and I was seeing more problems with my house than really existed. My mom had been trying to calm me down all week.

"Mom," I screamed. She came rushing down the stairs like it was the end of the world.

"What? What is it sweetie, what's wrong?" I didn't realize that my scream had been so intense. I adjusted my voice and tried again. "Mom, what are we going to eat tomorrow? Please, please, please try not to embarrass me. What are we going to do for dessert?"

My mom grabbed my shoulders and gave me small shake. "Emma, Emma! Calm down. It's just dinner. You'll be fine. We're having Pulled Pork sandwiches and I'm leaving dessert to you. Do whatever what you want." I couldn't believe this. I didn't cook. I didn't bake. In fact, anything in the kitchen was a bad idea for me and I avoided it to the best of my ability. How could she be doing this to me?

As I worried myself sick about dessert, the perfect idea popped into my head. I flipped open my phone and pushed down two. I was pretty sure Cindy was on every witch's speed dial and I had no problem calling her. I was after all her favorite cousin. At least that's what I told myself. Cousins were supposed to do things for each other.

As soon as she answered I told her my situation and she promised to make something new and refreshing and perfect. She said that she would even do it free of charge. This was why I loved her so much.

Now that that was dealt with, I was able to better focus. I grabbed a bagel off the counter and rushed down the street to make it to work on time. The kids all swarmed around me and we began our daily ritual. Joycie, a girl who I knew to by magically inclined, grabbed my hand and led me to a small corner of the room. "Emma," she said, "look what I can do."

Joycie pointed toward the drinking fountain at the other end of the room and closed her eyes in concentration. She whispered a spell under her breath, and liquid began seeping out of the bottom. Right before the stream hit the ground, it disappeared. I looked back down at the three-year old and she smiled up at me. "Just wait. I'm not done yet."

She held her hand palm up and a single drop of water appeared. She opened her mouth and another one dripped in as if from an invisible icicle. I was amazed. How was a three year old capable of collecting water and then storing it for when she needed it? It was incredible. There were a few other witches among the toddlers, but none of them had developed their power to this extent yet. I found myself sincerely wishing that Kassie was one of them.

The next night finally came around and Cindy had sent something as promised. Sam and his family came over and found myself relieved. We ate our Pulled Pork and talked then ate and talked some more. The dessert was delicious and everything went down beautifully.

Around ten o'clock, Sam mentioned that there was supposed to be a lunar eclipse around midnight and it seemed wrong not to watch it. I agreed and so our mothers decided that it was to be done. "Kassie's already asleep on the couch anyway, so we may as well."

Twelve o'clock came around at last and I led Sam out to the back yard. He immediately climbed up the steps of the trampoline and started jumping. "Come on Em, come join me." I shook my head and before I knew it he was on the ground beside me. He tossed me onto his shoulder and threw me on. I laughed as he climbed back up.

"You know it's not nice to force people to do things." He shrugged and I chuckled. The eclipse was just beginning and we sat close looking up at the red moon. As I watched the sky I was once again amazed at its immensity. I stole a glance at Sam's face and found that he was watching me intently. He smiled at me and I felt his hand touch mine. I looked down and flipped my hand over, giving him permission to hold it. Our fingers interlocked and then we both went back to looking at the sky.

At some point, I placed my head on his shoulder. I yawned and he gently picked me up and carried me off the trampoline. "I can walk," I said, mostly because I wanted to be on my feet when we kissed which I was sure would happen. He set me down and we made our way to the door. I tried to think of ways to get him to kiss me since I didn't have keys, so I couldn't do the whole Hitch thing. I eventually went with fiddling with my thumbs.

"Um, Emma," Sam stumbled.

"Yes."

"Tonight was really great." This was harder than I thought it would be. Sam was too much of a gentlemen to kiss me without my permission. I gave him a few more seconds to try to work out his feelings before I finally just took the initiative myself. I pressed my lips up against his, surprised that they knew what to do. But I guess love just had that ability.

When we pulled apart, Sam chuckled. "Wow," he said. "That was..."

"...good enough to try again," I finished for him. He wrapped his arms around my waist and leaned in. He went his ninety percent and then I finished with the final ten.

We kissed again and I felt his hand move up my body until his finger rested directly behind my ear. His hand wandered under my hair and then down my back. Suddenly, I felt it's coolness against my flesh. Both hands came around and pushed against my belly.

I suddenly really, really wanted him. I found myself searching for more skin and the extreme hunger I had for him scared me. His hands discovered the waistline of my jeans and I pulled away quickly. "What is it, Emma?" I shook my head, breathing hard.

"I want you Sam, I really do. But not like this, not here, not now." Dammit Emma, why do you have to be so pure, I asked myself, but at the same time something inside of me was very proud of my decision and I held onto that. I knew right and wrong, and I wasn't ready for this kind of relationship. Not to mention the curse that was rumored to be tied to premarital sex.

Sam took my hands and smiled at me. "Thank you," he said. I scrunched my eyebrows and he chuckled. "I don't know what came over me. That's not something I would ever do. Thank you for having the courage to back away." Wow, I thought. He doesn't care. He kissed me once again; a short sweet kiss on the cheek and I decided then that he absolutely could not be more perfect.

Stephan's Story by Peg Lewis

Dark halls lighted by candles! I tried to press my wispy white curls against the sides of my head but I couldn't see enough in the mirror to be sure what I was doing. And by my age I had learned to avoid squandering my Magic on such trivial needs.

Still, squinting because of the dark and leaning down from my awkward tallness to look in the mirror again, I pulled at a wayward ringlet and tucked it behind my ear. Stepping back, I checked my bearing: strong, in control, in my prime.

A pale figure passed quickly behind me, his (her?) footsteps muted by the thick carpet. The members were collecting.

I caught a scent of ... what? Cedar? The memories this scent evoked eluded me, something like walking in cool woods on a hot day.

I gathered my thoughts. The meeting would start very soon.

For whatever reason, I was nervous about this case and the meeting about to start. I wanted to make it go away. Why must the Council of Magic always interfere, always take umbrage at the slightest self-expression that deviated from the accepted use of Magic? Why was there no room for individuality?

Well, of course we were all highly individual, we recognized that. Some had powers others could barely discern or comprehend, while others of us were endowed with more showy forms of Magic.

And I, Stephan, certainly was in the forefront of those who wanted something universal to keep all these expressions of Magic under some sort of control, or self-expression could lead to mischief that would call undue attention from the Ordinary world.

I continued to wonder where the true balance lay between using our powers, our gifts I guess you could call them, and abusing our powers. I turned away from the mirror, and my inner reflections as well, and entered the chamber.

All stood. I quickly sat and motioned them all to their seats. All sat. That is, all sat but for the woman in white – someone I didn't know but who was no doubt the subject of our meeting. She! She alone remained standing.

She stared at me in a most disconcerting manner from the far end of the room.

I kept my gaze on her, hoping that my face was relaxed enough to disarm her attempts at intimidation. Surely it was intimidation she had in mind.

I pinched my forehead, hoping to remember the details of the case. I looked down at the notes that had been prepared for each committee member, myself included. Then I felt the chamber tremble and rumble. Or rather I heard it rumble. I looked up to see our guest smile smugly to herself as she sat down.

Surely that had been an earthquake.

My first thought was that she was taking the upper hand. No one could make an earthquake but a supremely capable, hugely powerful Earth witch! But then it had been just a rumble, no damage done, and from deep inside me came the thought, almost a tickle, that what I had just felt was almost a kind of flirtatious greeting.

I looked around me. A few of my fellow judges looked here and there uneasily, while others seemed oblivious of the quake.

I lowered my head again as if to study the papers in front of me. But my eyes were seeking out the face of the plaintiff. I wanted to know what she was up to, intimidation, perhaps anger? – or perhaps flirtation, came the thought.

Ridiculous, I retorted.

Certainly I knew the case from memory, now that she had given us a taste of what she had been accused of. Mischief! And as we could see, unabashed mischief! Hardly a penitent plaintiff!

I was surprised. The Council of Magic had traditionally had enough power that the very thought of being called before it was sufficient to intimidate the most daring.

So who was this woman sitting casually at the end of this august chamber, the one looking at her palm as if she were reading something there? The one smiling?

Miranda Duncan. Old royalty, it sounded like.

And oh yes. An Earth witch. Pretty much THE Earth witch. The greatest of all, some said. An intense Power among us, the powerful. And the one most likely to abuse her power, I thought as I looked through her record.

She appeared to be in her 40s, old enough to know that throwing her Magic around could cause permanent disruptions in the balance of Powers or even be verifiable by the Ordinaries. Enough unexplained perturbations and they would become certain of Magic and the most important line between us and them would begin to erode. Or be breached, just as bad.

In my 70 or so years in leadership positions, I had seen others of the Magic folk throw their craft around wantonly. I had seen selfish D'jinn and evil Centaurs break the ages-old basic principles that have kept the world structured and functional. I have seen young children discover their Magic too early, and teens rebel against the very concept of the rules just as they come into the full knowledge of their own powers.

But a witch in her 40s usually knew better. So why the rumbles, which really amounted to not much?

The committee members sat calmly facing me but I could feel the electricity in the air. After years of back and forth, we finally had the infamous Miranda before us for questioning. I stood and looked at each face lifted toward mine.

The process had gone smoothly. Miranda had been reprimanded by the committee. The committee had been ignored by Miranda, who had spoken not a word. She had been led out by the same officers who had brought her in, or their counterparts. Now it was time to deliberate.

I opened the discussion and listened to each argument. The indiscretion on the docket, which she had not denied, was of having too many husbands. It was unseemly and this gathering of a dozen utterly seemly and rather oldish and ordinary-seeming men predictably objected.

The irony had to do with the actual nature of the group: their Magic, collectively, transcended virtually every other power on Earth.

So I said, "What , are you afraid of irregularities among us? Who among us can honestly say he has been utterly discrete all his life?"

Every hand went up. Everyone looked deeply solemn.

Then the table began to shake.

It was not a violent shake.

The committee sat as one with their hands raised, looking dourly at me. The table drew the occasional sideways glance but no other signs of noticing it were forthcoming from the dozen.

I decided we should end these proceedings quickly. The plaintiff would need to repent of her wanton ways, and perhaps a simple confession would lay the whole matter to rest.

An electric sizzle in my brain caused my hands to twitch. Drat! The signal that I was slipping away from Truth was going off full volume.

The bailiff at the door waited. I looked around the room again. What had triggered that warning? What WAS the untruth I had thought?

Surely the facts of the case were known and in fact as we had just seen were undisputed. And my judgment that we should give her a barely noticeable slap on the wrist had plenty of precedent. So where had the untruth lain?

I wondered if I had been having a stroke instead of a warning of straying from the truth. But I felt fine.

I signaled the bailiff and he turned to the door to get the plaintiff. To get Miranda. I tensed myself against a possibility of the floor buckling or the table tipping over. I kept an eye on the door.

Neither bailiff nor Miranda appeared.

My anticipation rose. Who was this mischief-maker that she would toy with the highest council in the all the Magical realms? Because I was certain she had mischief on her mind.

The committee members were chatting among themselves. No one seemed in a rush, no one seemed to notice anything unusual.

I alone sat in my chair, disengaged from those around me, sweating. Miranda! Who was this witch?

The door opened. But no one appeared through it.

The others were still talking, sometimes bickering, amongst themselves. I got up and strode to the door, then peered around the corner.

Miranda stood there. A wisp of translucence. She motioned me into the hallway. All was dark and quiet there, with no one in sight, no bailiff nor any of the bustling staff that usually filled the halls.

I went. She stopped. She was taller than I had thought. I barely had to look down at her.

She moved closer to me. I couldn't move my feet. My arms entwined her. Her sigh felt like a fresh breeze, cool and exquisitely refreshing.

She kissed me. She smelled like roses, like jasmine, like mint, like cloves. Her hands brushed lightly against my face. The wind from her breath blew my curls into disarray. Her face was lighted like the palest of full moons. Her eyes opened like black poppies hit by sunlight. Her embrace was strong and firm.

We were just out of the candlelight. I could sense the committee members leaving the chambers. Friends in groups of two or three talked in hush tones or shared a moment of levity.

The chastisement, the hearing, the seeds of intolerance and fear had evaporated from them all.

And I could feel it all slipping from my mind. I chased a few responsibilities as they fell away from conscious thought, then willingly let them go.

They were replaced by Miranda, she who filled my chaste soul with longing and fulfillment, both.

The candle dripped its last and sputtered. Still we stood entangled body and soul.

Then we were running barefoot across cool grass toward the rising sun. And that was the end of night for me.

Made in the USA
Las Vegas, NV
01 March 2021